Capital Crimes

SEP 0 4 2012

Capital Crimes

15 Tales by Sacramento Area Authors

Edited by
Kathleen L. Asay and Patricia E. Canterbury

Introduction by
Gabrielle Guedet

Foreword by
Robin Burcell

Capital Crimes: 15 Tales by Sacramento Area Authors,
by members of Capitol Crimes,
the Sacramento Chapter of Sisters in Crime.
**Copyright © 2008 by Capitol Crimes,
the Sacramento Chapter of Sisters in Crime.**
All rights reserved.

The following are included in this anthology by permission of the respective authors:

Foreword, Robin Burcell.

Introduction, Gabrielle Guedet

"The Breaking Story," Kathleen L. Asay

"The Case of Xu Chen," Patricia E. Canterbury

"Give the Devil His Due," Juanita J. Carr

"In the Pocket of a Dead Man," SM Caruthers

"Storm Warnings," Geri Spencer Hunter

"The Award," R. Franklin James

"Playing House," Teresa Judd

"Smoke Trail," Norma Lehr

"Beneath Cherry Trees," Nan Mahon

"Digital," Joyce Mason

"Reunion," Patt Gilman

"Tea Time," Cindy Sample

"Doggie Style Dead," Linda Joy Singleton

"In Search of Millie," Nancy Streukens

"Borrowed Time," Dänna Suzanne Wilberg

FIRST EDITION

ISBN: 978-0-6151-8508-8

Published by

Umbach Consulting
6966 Sunrise Blvd., #263
Citrus Heights, California 95610

Member, Citrus Heights Chamber of Commerce and
Northern California Publishers & Authors

For information: info@umbachconsulting.com or 916-733-2159

Book design and cover photo of the California State Capitol by
Kenneth W. Umbach and used by permission.

Printed in U.S.A.

Foreword

Robin Burcell[*]

The short story is a form of literature I have long admired, and so I was eager to read what our fine group of Sacramento writers put together. What I discovered was that reading this anthology was very much like walking into a small and intimate art gallery. Like any gallery, there is something for everyone. From cozy to creepy, traditional to noir, you'll find a vast assortment of stories between these covers.

Something to keep in mind about this particular mystery genre is that the writer has a limited number of pages in which to ensure the gist of the story, and not every story has the same message. Good doesn't necessarily triumph over evil, humor is sometimes skewed, justice isn't necessarily blind, or even fair. Each writer has something very different to say, and does so in his or her own fashion. It is, in fact, what I love about the art of short stories. One can appreciate the subtleties of one, the broad strokes of another. Some have a satisfying end, others are twisted, meant to leave you thinking. What they all offer is a slice of life, be it for good or evil. So come, take a walk through our gallery, or rather, sit back, relax, and most of all . . . enjoy.

[*] Award-winning mystery author Robin Burcell's *The Face of a Killer* is to be published in 2008. Previous novels include *Fatal Truth* and Anthony award nominee *Every Move She Makes*.

Contents

Introduction: How We Started

Gabrielle Guedet[†]

It was not a dark and stormy night. It was a sunny, pleasant Saturday in October 1995. I walked into the pizza parlor on Florin Road, eager to attend the first meeting of the Sacramento Chapter of Sisters in Crime (SinC). A woman ahead of me was asking the question I was hoping to ask, "Where is the Sisters in Crime meeting?" I could tell by the baffled expression on the man's face that we were in the wrong place. I stepped up and mentioned that we had been told that the meeting would take place at the Round Table on Florin. He informed us of another Round Table on the other side of the freeway. Geri Spencer Hunter and I walked out together and got into our respective cars, drove across the freeway, and found the correct Round Table.

When we entered the pizza parlor and asked our question, we were directed to the back room. There sat Jacqueline Turner Banks, Terris McMahon Grimes, and Patricia E. Canterbury. "Welcome to Sisters in Crime" they greeted. I sat down next to Geri, happy to finally be in a local chapter. I had been a member of SinC since 1989 and had never had a local chapter to join, until then.

On that Saturday, I had recently returned from the 26th Annual Bouchercon mystery convention, which had been held

---

[†] Brief biographies of all contributors to this volume begin on page 173.

in Nottingham, England. I was eager to tell the new membership of the upcoming 28th Bouchercon to be held in Monterey, California. We went through introductions, each of us in turn answering the question, "Are you a mystery writer or a mystery reader or both?" When it got to my turn I explained that I was an avid reader who had been corrupted by a nun when I was 15. But that I had some important information about the Bouchercons that the membership could benefit from. "What is a Bouchercon?" was the response. I explained about the Bouchercon, named after famed mystery writer Anthony Boucher, and the annual breakfast meeting held by SinC at these meetings. I told the other attendees of the wonders of being in a group of people, usually 2000 or more, who really loved the mystery genre. I told them of the opportunity to help with the 28th Bouchercon, to be held in Monterey, and gave them the important contact phone numbers and other information.

Our chapter continued to meet at that same pizza parlor for some time. We did participate in the 28th Bouchercon. Jackie, Terris, Pat, and I shared the presidency several times. Our chapter has grown and has now produced its very own anthology. The first idea for an anthology came after I came back from another Bouchercon carrying an anthology put together by the San Luis Obispo Chapter. I asked the membership if we couldn't try one of our own. Since that time several other chapters have published their own anthologies, and now we get to join their ranks.

I hope you enjoy these wonderful stories by members of the Sacramento Chapter of Sisters in Crime. We have certainly enjoyed gathering them together to present to you. Reading mysteries is a wonderful way to spend a day.

The Breaking Story

Kathleen L. Asay

I was speeding up a ramp to the Costa Mesa freeway, bound for my desk at the *Orange County Star-Bulletin*, when I caught a breaking story on the all-news radio station. It was the sort of story that excites news programmers so the station even had a reporter on the scene calling the action.

"—The bulldozers are here. There are two of them along with a machine with jaws like a T-Rex. Dump trucks are standing by. They planned to begin clearing this area today.

"The marshals have already served notice. It's up to the Eberly family now. Sheriff's officers will go in if they don't come out on their own.

"Yes, I can see a woman and two children now. They're holding hands as they come down the driveway. The spectators behind me are cheering. But the woman keeps looking back. There's no sign of her husband.

"The county has said it won't let a single landowner stand in the way of the development that is planned for these hills. They have already condemned this stretch, which is where the road will go. The landowner, John Eberly, will retain the rest of his property, including where his house stands, though the new road will come within fifty yards of the house. Eberly told the county he would fight. Now it comes down to this. The family is walking out. Eberly is not in sight."

I took the next off ramp, rolled through the red and sped back onto the freeway heading north. The office could wait; I had to see where this one went.

John Eberly was my "mountain man." Not mine exactly, but he felt like mine. My "Eye on the County" column had landed his name and cause on breakfast tables across Orange County. I wrote the column because his kind of commitment moved me, and because he had lost. Now, instead of conceding, it appeared he had taken the fight to new ground, physical ground, and sent his wife and children out.

My foot trembled on the accelerator, looking for breaks in the traffic. I shot off two ramps later and drove east toward hills that had yet to turn green in a drier than normal January. Traffic thinned and commerce gave way to housing, sporadic acres of stucco, tile and infantile trees surrounded by scrub grass, the last vestiges of the past fast disappearing to the sounds of hammers and earth-movers as the building continued.

"The stand-off," said the radio reporter, "has been going on now for several hours. About eight thirty this morning when the trucks arrived, a shot was fired from the house toward the bulldozers. Sheriff's officers were called in and the stand-off began. A few minutes ago, a woman and two children left the house. According to a spokesman for the sheriffs, her husband, identified as John Eberly, is thought to have remained inside and to be armed and dangerous. If he wanted attention, he's got it now from reporters and spectators here in the canyon and media helicopters overhead.

"The Eberlys live on about twenty acres up Rialto Canyon, where he says he's created a preserve of native plants and animals that this road will destroy. The county has decreed the road necessary to the development of Rialto Vista, and says the road has been on the county plan for years. Eberly should have known this when he bought his land. An argument between Eberly and Bruce Covington, the developer, erupted at the last supervisors' meeting when the go-ahead was given for the road work."

The cars ahead of me and coming toward me made the same turn I did onto Rialto Canyon Road: spectators and TV and print news, perhaps John's biggest audience yet. The road wound more tightly as the hills grew steeper. At the bottom of the canyon, random houses fit as snugly into the narrow basin as the trees overhanging the road. I'd looked at the houses more carefully on my first trip up the canyon. I'd seen wood clapboard a hundred years old and the dull sheen of Airstream trailers, laundry on lines strung from trees and sculpture gardens of stone, burlwood and the rusted remains of abandoned automobiles. Sometimes the road turned so sharply you felt you might roll right up a gravel driveway into a house. Other times, you got caught looking, wondering, and nearly went the other way, into the rocky bed of the winter creek.

The people who lived up that canyon and ones like it sided with John. They wanted their canyon to remain as it was, a last refuge for the independent spirit to make its own way without comment or complaint from government or neighbor. Now government and vast numbers of potential neighbors threatened to overrun their refuge.

But what had drawn out the crowds was the scent of blood.

Capital Crimes

I followed the cars making the slow winding climb up the canyon. At some point we entered the Santa Ana Mountains; south and east from here was the Cleveland National Forest, which was not a forest like those of the higher Sierra but a drier browner version. The air smelled of oak and sage and knee high dry grass. Occasionally a sinew of water could be seen in the creek, shining on the sandstone and glinting between the trees.

The cars ahead of me stopped abruptly. We were at least a hundred yards from where the dirt lane that was John's driveway met Rialto Canyon Road. Another hundred yards further, the road ended. There the bulldozers would work to extend the road up the canyon to the ridge that would someday be home to five hundred families, Rialto Vista. From the top of the ridge, according to developers, you could see Catalina Island.

Not very often, I would argue, though I had seen the lights of coastal Newport from John's deck. I had also seen the scraped hillsides and the new tile roofs marching eastward, coming closer as they would each day. He had wanted me to see that so I would understand. I looked into a rabbit's hole with his children and ate squash pie for dinner with the family. Dinner had come entirely from the Eberly garden. Later, John and I stood on the deck and looked at the lights. I asked him what he would do if he lost.

"Well, I won't lie down in front of the bulldozers," he had said, dry, ironic. "That's what they expect in the city. Then the cops come along and haul the protestors into court, and by the time you get out, the damage has been done. Well, not here. That's not the way we do things out here. You know?"

I hadn't, but I did not pursue the question. I'd been a little afraid of the answer, a failing, I now knew. I had thought I could wait. Maybe the county would side with John.

Of course, they had not. Two days after my visit to John's house, I watched my mountain man square off against a smiling Bruce Covington, our county's biggest developer. Covington was a winner because he knew how to smile at politicians, the press and even the opposition. John, uncomfortable in a suit and tie, had chafed at the trappings of civilization. Finally unable to contain himself, he erupted from his chair shouting like a child trying to get the attention of adults.

"You want to see Catalina," he snapped, "take the damn boat."

County officials recoiled, but Bruce Covington's easy political smile only tightened slightly. A deputy on duty in the chamber restrained John and told him politely, but succinctly, that if he could not control his outbursts, he would be removed. John squirmed for the next hour, ranted when it was his turn to talk and ultimately left the meeting shouting that he would fight their decision. I went back to work that night and wrote my column.

Less than two weeks later, I was angling my car into the dirt at the side of the road like the others before me, ready to make the hike to see what John would do. As I walked, I rummaged in my handbag for my press identification and hung the plastic tags around my neck.

From the shade of the canyon road, we entered the bold sunlight of the clearing for the unmarked lane that was the entrance to the Eberly property. Sheriff's deputies and their vehicles formed the front lines behind which stood the reporters and gawkers. In the distance, heavy equipment and trucks labeled Covington Homes stood abandoned. A sheriff's helicopter traced a low circle overhead. Higher, two news service helicopters made slow passes.

Instead of pushing through the crowd, I cut a long trail around, over boulders and through the trees. Dressed for an early morning interview, my clothes were all wrong: low suede boots, a split skirt of brown wool the color of fresh humus, a layering of sweaters in terra cotta, and hammered copper jewelry. I was too warm and the boots fashionable but useless. The jewelry and the press tags clanked.

Of all the people there, however, I was fairly certain I was one of the few who had actually been there before. I knew, for instance, that beyond the fifty yards of dense growth that paralleled the creek up to the house, there was open grassland, the family vegetable garden and the chicken coop. I knew John was not on the deck, which we could see above the trees, but in the half-basement, a lean, sun-hardened radical in his early forties looking back at us like a guerilla warrior through below ground windows.

The sheriff's department had sent its SWAT team, not all perhaps, but enough to quell a small revolution. They had rifles with impressive sights, state of the art radios and paramilitary uniforms; they did not look kind or forgiving. They held the crowd back, pointed uphill and plotted. When reporters tried to talk to them, they shook their heads, grunted and walked away. The reporters chatted among themselves, and everyone tried to talk to Mrs. Eberly who stood with her children clutched against her, staring at her home so thoroughly under siege.

It was nine year old Jason Eberly who spotted me and broke the stalemate at the front lines.

"Celie!" he said. He broke from his mother and ran to grab my arm. "You have to stop them. They're going to kill my dad!"

I worked my way, his hand in mine, through the brush to the tree where his mother stood like a statue. Susan was a strong woman, I already knew, a full partner to her husband both physically and mentally. She wore jeans, leather boots, a work shirt, no make up or jewelry. Drop her in Fashion Island and people would stare. In the canyon, we were the ones who looked out of place, unprepared for the weather and the terrain. She watched my arrival with no change in her expression. "Cecilia," she said, an acknowledgement rather than a greeting. She would see where I stood first.

The reporters and the uniforms went quiet.

I sighed, shook my head and turned so I could look toward the house.

"Celie!" said Jason. Lindsey, the younger child, whimpered against her mother's knee.

"It's up to your dad," I said to Jason.

"They haven't any right to be here," he said.

"They think they do. And your dad shot at them, didn't he? He shouldn't have done that."

"But they were on our land!"

"That's no excuse."

"Yes, it is!"

"Hush," said Susan.

"You know these people?" asked a uniform.

"A little," I said.

"Over here."

Like, Come over here, please. I followed with a heavy heart, feeling the grass and dirt penetrate my boots and irritate my feet. A bead of sweat rolled down my face near my ear, the sweat of fear as much as heat.

He led me aside and through the ranks of deputies to a car where another officer slouched against the hood, a telephone against his ear, a bored, dissatisfied look on his face. My presence did nothing to change that. I watched him total me up: suede boots, handmade jewelry, press tags. A bleeding liberal. On hearing I knew the family, his frown deepened. Still, he was the one on the phone because someone thought he could talk to snipers or hostage takers, which in his mind was probably not all that different from talking to a member of the press.

"You want to try?" he asked.

I shuddered. He took that for agreement.

"There's a lady here," he said into the phone, "Cecilia Mas Lamb," reading from my I.D., and saying "Ceceelia" in mock Spanish.

He held the phone out. "Man wants to talk."

I took the receiver with a sweaty hand and brushed away another line of sweat from my cheek before I spoke.

"Hello, John," I said.

"So you're there, too."

"You're on the radio. Half of Orange County is here. They're shopping for home sites."

He laughed. Sharp, penetrating. I closed my eyes.

"Did I kill anyone down there?"

"No."

"Too bad."

"John."

"Yeah?"

"Let it go."

"Just when it's getting interesting?"

"It's not getting interesting. It's getting damned dangerous. There are sharpshooters behind every tree between here and Riverside. Give it up. Please. If you do, you'll still have something, but if you don't, your family will have nothing."

"They'll know I stood up for it. They'll have that."

"No one stands in the way of progress. No one."

"You mean no one stands in the way of Bruce Covington."

"He's only the leading edge. If not him, someone else."

"And here I thought if I stopped Covington, I could stop them all."

"John—"

"Yeah. I know. But if I come out, what fine words will you write about me? 'He gave up?'"

"'He lived.'"

"Shit, Cecilia. Who'd want to?"

I shivered in spite of the heat and wished I was still on the freeway, headed for the office. "Please. If you don't, I won't ever come and look for rabbit holes with your kids again."

Silence. A long break. I waited. Tears mixed with sweat on my face. The telephone was slippery in my hand. The cops shifted feet, made small noises of impatience.

"John—" I said again.

"Yeah," he returned. "Tell them yeah."

"I will."

"Yeah." He slammed down the receiver. Downstairs phone, I thought. Now he's on his way upstairs. What will he do with the gun? Which gun? I handed the telephone back to the officer who had given it to me and he frowned when he realized John had hung up.

"He's coming out," I said.

His frown turned into a smile without warmth, the smile of a man holding the winning hand in a game of poker. His other hand carried a radio. He spoke into it, "He's coming out."

From where we stood, I could see the house through the trees, the sunlight on the windows, the dark brown of the deck and siding, a spot of yellow that I thought was a flower pot. I had said there were sharpshooters behind every tree, but I hoped that was an exaggeration. I saw two, their weapons braced, aimed uphill. Otherwise, I was too far down, safe in the peanut gallery unable to see the stage, that lower door where John would appear. The men beside me waited, tense. The crowd stood their vigil, utterly quiet now. I recalled John's anger and frustration at the supervisors' meeting, his shouts for attention. Instead of feeling relief, dread chilled me to the bone. I wished I could see what was happening.

"There he is!" someone shouted. The guns moved. The canyon split open like it had been rocked by dynamite.

"NO!"

I'd screamed.

Deputies ran toward the house and the crowd surged around me and the Eberly family. I turned to see that Susan Eberly had not moved. She remained frozen as she had been, expressionless, her hands shielding her children's faces against her. When I moved to stand in front of her, her unseeing gaze slowly sharpened into focus.

"Why did he have to come to the house, Cecilia?" she asked, so low at first I barely heard her over the din, then stronger. "He was so cheerful. My husband is a proud man. He couldn't— He couldn't let another man win, not smiling like that. You understand, don't you?"

I tried to nod but all I managed was a small jerking movement. Her chin rose.

"Tell the police to look in the barn. Mr. Covington will not see his homes built, after all. I did what I could, Cecilia. I kept the children from seeing."

———

"David caught the story," Nina, my editor, said. David was from News, an old hand and a good one. He and a cameraman had arrived soon after I had so there were pictures, too, of Susan and her kids and the stretchers bearing out what was left of John Eberly and Bruce Covington. Covington had decided to make one last gesture of appeasement and had been shot for his troubles, an hour before the bulldozers arrived.

"David'll need the details of what went down from your angle," Nina added. "Then we want the personal from you, your feelings about the man and what the hell he thought he was doing. Emotional stuff. We'll run them together. Companion pieces, front page. There'll be an investigation into both shootings. Bell is working that.

"Cecilia?"

"I could use some coffee."

"Sure," she said, too bright.

She was young. She still believed in rabbit holes.

The Case of Xu Chen
A Tanner Sullivan Mystery

Patricia E. Canterbury

My name is Tanner Sullivan. I'm a detective, much to the shame of my family. Yes, I'm that Tanner Sullivan, the one who graduated from Stanford in 1919 with a degree in economics and was going to set the world of business on its ear. A 6'3", 210 pound colored man who was the privileged grandson of Abner Beaureguard Sullivan could do no less. My grandfather had made a small fortune off the miners during the gold rush and by selling supplies to the Chinese who lived in and around Weed, California. Everyone thought I would go into the family banking business and open a branch office in San Francisco after I returned from my grand tour of Europe. At the beginning of the 20th Century, everyone with means, regardless of color, went to Europe, and I was no different. The trip was to be my final fling before delving into the mysterious and challenging world of banking and commerce.

I was in Paris when my favorite cousin, Anna, disappeared. She had gone to San Francisco to find a suitable building for our bank; three weeks later, the last person to see her was a Chinese dressmaker working late in a laundry on Stockton Street. By the time I returned home, all traces of her were gone. I gave up all thoughts of banking, rented a two room flat in

Chinatown, got my private investigator's license, and opened an office just down the street from the laundry. Anna's still missing after nearly eleven years, but I know that I will find her someday.

This story is about Xu Chen and the men who may one day lead me to Anna.

It was 1930 on a typical San Francisco summer day, cold, with fog hovering around the corners of my building as if it were afraid to venture out into the streets. The building is a half block from North Beach. I can hear the foghorns and the cries of seagulls, and the Powell Street cable car clangs as it rounds a corner a few blocks away. I don't have to go looking for trouble or adventure; both know the way to my office. So I was at my desk waiting for the telephone to ring or for someone to walk in off the streets, like the elderly, bent, Chinese woman who burst into my inner office that day.

I looked behind her to find out what had happened to Sally Fong, my usually reliable secretary. Sally brings in many elderly Chinese who are too afraid of the Tong to speak to the cops and I help find whoever is missing. They trust me because of my family history. I grew up in Weed, a place steeped in the history of Chinese and colored families dating back to the 1840s.

I expected to see Sally, but the outer office was empty.

Before I could ask the old woman a question, she said, "You find him. Xu Chen missing." Then she began to cry. Perhaps, cry is too strong a word. Her eyes filled with tears and the tears ran slowly down her small wrinkled face and dripped onto her yellow silk dress, leaving small tear stains on the fabric. She didn't make a sound. It was eerie. I'm used to women who shout when they cry. The whole neighborhood hears them. This old woman cried as if crying were something foreign to her.

"Have a seat," I said. "Can I get you something?" I looked at the bottle of gin on the top of the bookshelf behind her. 10:30 in the morning was too early for gin. Besides it was illegal and she could be an undercover cop. I smiled at the joke.

"Water?" I was looking around for a clean glass when Sally entered the outer office. She looked over at the old woman, frowned and walked toward my office. Sally's used to seeing elderly Chinese seated in one of the client's chairs. Usually she's the one ushering them in. From the look on her face, this old woman was not one of Sally's charges.

"Sally, get her a cup of coffee, please. No, make it tea," I said, as I sat on the edge of my desk to face our guest.

"Who is Xu Chen?" I asked.

The old woman looked at me and frowned as if she were translating my words from English to Mandarin and back again.

"What?" Her voice sounded like roses on silk, soft, delicate, refined like her tears.

"Xu Chen. You asked if I could find him. Who is he?"

"Not, who, what." Now it was my turn to frown.

Sally reentered my office with a steaming pot of tea.

"Madge next door already had a pot brewing," she said, in answer to my unasked question. "She has a china set. Four cups and saucers plus a really old pot."

I nodded. What I knew about teapots I could put in a thimble. I'm a detective, as I said before and a dammed good one. I find those who are missing or don't want to be found, everyone, that is, but Anna. I guessed Mrs. Chen wanted me to find her husband, Xu Chen. Rather than guess, I decided to ask.

"Mrs. Chen, is it your husband that you wish me to find?" I said, as the old woman sipped from the rose colored bone china teacup. It was difficult to determine which was older or more delicate.

She looked up at me through eyes older than the hills of San Francisco.

"I'm not Mrs. Chen. My name . . . Mei Yung," she said, haltingly. Strange, one minute she appeared to understand and speak perfect English, then questions formed on her face. What's going on, I thought but I didn't ask.

Instead I said, "Mrs. Yung, who is Xu Chen?"

"She is my starling."

"Starling?" Sally and I asked in unison. I'd forgotten that Sally was still in the room.

"Yes, starling. Bird. Do you understand?"

"Yes, but I'm a detective. I find missing people. You have to check with the SPCA or the Sierra Club."

"Audubon," Sally interrupted.

"The Audubon," I repeated.

"No," the old woman shouted. "It must be you. I was told you . . . the best," she insisted but in a softer tone as if she were remembering that she was an old woman.

"At finding people," I said, trying to hide my smile. "I don't know anything about starlings."

"Find Xu Chen. I pay." She opened a small green silk purse and took out an even smaller yellow silk coin purse. From that she extracted a dollar sized red jade stone that she placed into my palm. I knew that a jade piece that size and that color must be worth a fortune.

I heard myself saying, "I—I can't accept this."

"Is it not enough?"

"It's too much."

"Nothing too much for Xu Chen."

In that case, I needed to know more about the bird.

"Sally, take this down," I said as Mrs. Yung described her pet. Again her words were halting. The internal translation, I thought.

"She is . . . beautiful. Dark . . . gray and brown with red tips on her wings. She is a . . . quiet thing. I much like." She sniffed into her handkerchief then took a sip of the tea. It had to be cold by now. Sally sensed my thoughts and picked up the cup as soon as it was placed back on my desk.

"I'll get you a refill."

Mei Yung turned and waited until Sally was out of the office.

"You must find her. Now." Her small fingers fastened onto my arm and held it in a vise-like grip. I was amazed that someone so small had fingers that strong. I could feel my arm going numb.

"Okay, okay. I'll look for her," I said. Mei Yung released her grip and smiled. She quickly turned her head toward the door as Sally re-entered, but she wasn't quick enough to hide the smile. The one I saw was not that of a frail old woman worried about a lost pet. No, it was the smile of a predator.

I spent the next week checking pet stores, walking through Golden Gate Park and listening to bird songs along the ocean.

Capital Crimes

The homeless folks who had taken up residence in the park were too hungry to notice the coming and going of birds and I saw no dark brown feathers stuck in the whiskers of the feral cats. I even visited the SPCA. To say that I was laughed out the door would have been an understatement. Desperate, I had lunch with my old friend Miles Archer. His partner, Sam Spade, was in Monterey on a case. Both of them are good detectives. Sometimes Miles sees things that I don't, even though I'm better, especially when it comes to dealing with the Chinese. Miles laughed.

"Tanner, who'd a thought. A bird. Gimme a break. No one's crazy enough to go looking for a damn bird."

I had to admit it was crazy.

Another day passed. I was almost ready to throw in the towel when I saw five men nearly as old as Mei Yung walking down Powell Street. Each carried an empty birdcage in one hand and a small paper box in the other. They spoke rapidly to each other.

Ah ha, I thought, birdmen. If I followed them, I might learn where else to look for a lost starling. They turned into the Imperial Tea Court on Powell. I followed.

The Tearoom was filled on one side with teapots of various shapes and sizes. In front of the counter were canisters of loose tea. But what caught my eye were the birdcages hanging from the ceiling on long, elaborate, braided brocade ropes. Most of the cages were empty; two contained birds. I sat at a table near the door and watched as the birdmen took tiny birds from the paper boxes and placed them into hand carved cages. The shopkeeper, a mere girl with long black braids wearing traditional

Chinese dress, set a tiny white-lidded cup in front of me and handed me a listing of four types of tea. I knew even less about teas than I did about tea pots. I pointed at something called "Monkey picked tikuanyin." She smiled and left with my order. I turned toward the nearest bird man.

"What kind of birds are those?" I asked the old man.

"Starling." Good, he spoke English. My conversational Mandarin was rusty but I could get my point across if I tried.

"You bring them to the tearoom?" I asked.

"Yep, everyday. We have tea together." He pointed at his companions.

"May I look at the cages?"

He pushed his cage, which was still on the table, toward me.

I couldn't believe the art work. Now, as I've said before, I'm a detective. Most people think of us as hard-nosed, no-nonsense people who bring in those who don't want to be brought in. But I have a soft side and I appreciate beautiful workmanship.

The cage was made of cherry wood and each bird feeder was hand-made porcelain with tiny dragons, flowers and mountains painted in blue on the sides. But what intrigued me were the hand-carved monkeys, dragons, tigers, and pandas that were the clasps for the doors or that held the perches. As I marveled at the tiny carvings, I heard a bird sing. It was the loudest sound I'd heard in days.

I looked up and there in a small cage near the back was a tiny brown and gray bird with red tips on its wings, singing away.

"Oh, my, Xu Chen," I said.

"You know Xu Chen?" the man whose cage I was admiring asked.

"Yes. No. I— Someone asked me to find her," I stammered. I couldn't believe it. I'd spent days looking for a bird that was right around the corner from my office and in a cage yet.

"Find her? She isn't missing. She belongs to my granddaughter. But she is not the one singing. Only the males sing," he said, smiling at my ignorance.

"Xu Chen belongs to your granddaughter?"

"Yes."

"Do you know Mei Yung?"

The old man's face clouded over. His companions, who had joined in the laughter at my expense, grew silent.

"Mei Yung. How do you know her?" Hatred burned in the old man's eyes.

"She came to my office and asked me to find her pet." I pulled out my card and handed it to the old man. He showed it to his companions. While we were speaking, the shopkeeper took a hooked pole, pulled the cage containing Xu Chen down and put a cover over it. Then she disappeared with the cage into the rear of the store. When I got up to follow her, the old men blocked my way for a moment.

"Xu Chen belongs to me," the old man shouted. "She is not for sale. Not now. Not ever. You tell Mei Yung that all the jade in China and America are not enough for Xu Chen."

I pushed past the men and went to the rear of the store. The back door opened onto an alley. The alley was empty.

Two more days passed before I heard from Mei Yung. I called the number she'd given me, but the person who answered didn't or wouldn't speak English. In halting Mandarin, I asked for Mei Yung. The phone went dead. I rang again, mentioned Mei Yung and another person hung up but not before I left my number.

I was in my office when Sally yelled, "Tanner, Mrs. Yung's on the phone."

"Mrs. Yung—" I began.

"Cut the crap," she said. "Where's the bird? I heard that you found it on Powell Street." Ah ha. So the delicate, confused woman from earlier in the month had been replaced with the Mei Yung the old men knew. This Mei Yung's voice was hard. I couldn't imagine her shedding tears over anyone or anything.

"I was told the bird belonged to a young girl."

"She is mine. I paid for her. Some simpleton gave her away to a child. I want the bird back. Now."

"Since you know that I was at the Imperial Tea Room, you also know that Xu Chen got away. I haven't found it. Nor have I found the old man who says that the bird belongs to his grand-daughter. You paid me a small fortune to find Xu Chen. I found it. Our partnership is done."

"You were to bring it to me."

"That's not what I agreed to do. I said I would look for it."

Again, I found myself speaking to the dial tone. Mei Yung had hung up. Okay, Tanner, what is so important about this bird that a very clever woman is paying a lot of jade to have you bring it to her? Why the helpless old woman act? I'm sure that my name reached all the corners of Chinatown; she would know that once I agreed to do something, I would follow through.

I sat at my desk, then got up, opened the gin bottle and poured two fingers into a coffee cup. Why had Mei Yung come to my office? Why had she said the bird was female, then male? Why did the birdmen know about Mei Yung?

I looked at the clock: Nearly 4:30.

I put on my fedora and raccoon coat and told Sally I'd see her in the morning. Outside, the fog that had hung around all day was heavier and thicker. I decided to go to the waterfront. Maybe the salt air would clear my head.

The pier was busy. Two ships were receiving cargo. I looked up and saw Mei Yung getting out of a taxi. She didn't see me. The man with her was a well-known leader of the Stockton Street Tong. He helped her step over a cargo rope and up the gangplank of a Chinese ship.

I tried to follow them but a man the size of a small house blocked my way. I reached for my identification and woke up lying in the gutter. I never saw the blow coming.

"Tanner, what brings you down to the docks?" asked Horace O'Brien, San Francisco's finest beat cop and my close friend. "Little early to be sleeping in the streets."

I rubbed my aching jaw and struggled to my feet.

"I'm on a case," I managed to say without spitting out half of my teeth. "I was following someone."

"Case, huh? Who ya trying to find?"

"Mei Yung—" I began.

Even in the semi-darkness I could see the color drain from O'Brien's face.

"Mei Yung's a hard case. She's the mother of Young Yip."

Young Yip was well known to the cops. He liked the opium dens and California Street whores. He also liked to beat up women. I think he has something to do with my Cousin Anna's disappearance but I can't prove it. My mind wandered. Thinking made my head hurt.

"We know that she's smuggling something out of the country soon, but we don't know what it is," he whispered as he steered me toward the middle of the street. O'Brien continued speaking while I tried to sort out Mei Yung, Xu Chen, old bird men and me. Why had she come to me?

"What?" O'Brien asked.

"Oh, I didn't realize I'd said it out loud. I asked why Mei Yung came to me."

"She came to see you?"

"Yes, something about finding a pet bird."

"Xu Chen. I know all about it. All of us down here do. It seems this really rare singing female bird, supposedly the only singing female of its kind, was given away to Tommy Sung's daughter. Even Mei Yung isn't crazy enough to go after anything of Tommy Sung's. I heard she'd hired someone to get the bird. I didn't know it was you. Boy, you're in deep."

I'd stopped listening when O'Brien mentioned Tommy Sung. Tommy was the head of the Powell Street Tong, the most ruthless tong members in San Francisco, and to think that I'd sat right next to his Pop, admiring his birdcage. Damn and I call myself a detective.

O'Brien was right; this was something between Tommy and Mei Yung. No way was I going to get involved.

Capital Crimes

A week later, Mei Yung's body was discovered in her stateroom aboard the China Star. The *San Francisco Examiner*'s obituary pages ran a small article about her death, but nothing more. I went to the coroner's office. Wilson Jones has cut some corners for me in the past. Perhaps there was something he could tell me about the way she died.

"Sorry, Tanner," Wilson said. "Looks like natural causes. She was an old woman. I can't find anything unusual."

Her son, Young Yip, disappeared.

Tommy Sung, seen near the Powell Street family laundry, was questioned and released.

I don't believe in coincidences so I found it mighty strange that Mei Yung died after asking me to find a special bird. No, there was more to this case than I was being told.

I went to the Imperial Tea Room to pick up a package of Monkey Picked tikuanyin. I'd grown quite found of it, especially mixed with two fingers of gin. Mr. Sung and his old friends were there. In a teak birdcage, singing for all to hear, was Xu Chen. A girl who looked to be about four years of age sat on Mr. Sung's lap clapping and giggling.

I purchased my tea, bowed at Mr. Sung and his friends and walked outside. I never did figure out why Mei Yung chose me. Was it fate, karma or dumb luck?

I turned my coat collar down; the sun was beginning to burn off the fog. It was going to be a beautiful day. Perhaps this would be the day that I'd find Anna.

Give the Devil His Due

Juanita J. Carr

Michael David Carver, known to everyone as Mick, pulled the dusty curtain aside and stared out his office window without interest. He was only vaguely aware of the traffic flowing up and down South Sacramento's Stockton Boulevard. Thoughts of Elaine were too fresh and painful; Mick's tan face was a picture of abject despair. Losing her had been like losing the sun, and knowing he was solely responsible only increased his agony. She had stuck by him for three years until his insatiable gambling drove her away. Now his decrepit office was another sorry reminder of his slide to the bottom. He wondered if thirty-five was too young to be deemed a failure.

A black stretch limo pulled boldly to the curb in a no parking zone outside his window. A slow smile tugged at the corners of his mouth, a welcome interest stirring in his imagination, proof that he was alive and well despite his downhill tumble. Eyeing the limo, he squashed the envy rising to taunt him, the little voice reminding him that he too could have owned luxury cars or any other material goods he desired if he had stopped gambling sooner. He craved a cigarette to puff away his disgust over the way his life had suddenly plummeted and futilely searched his shirt pocket until he remembered that he had given up smoking several months ago to please Elaine.

Cursing softly, he returned his attention to the scene outside his office and his entire body shook with disbelief when he saw

27

the chauffeur extract an elderly man from the rear seat and begin to walk with him towards his office. Mick swept his hand over his unruly brown hair and self consciously rubbed his unshaven face. Rabid curiosity raked his nerves raw as he left the window to stand behind his desk.

The ancient bell above the door tinkled as the chauffeur and the old man slowly entered the one room office. Mick's mouth froze in a parody of a welcome smile when he suddenly recognized his visitor. He quickly left his desk and made a half hearted gesture toward the sagging sofa, stunned to find himself playing host to Maynard Blakely, one of Sacramento's wealthiest patrons. Recovering from his initial shock, Mick began to speculate why a rich mogul would visit a down-and-out private detective, but he could think of no logical reason and soon gave it up.

Maynard Blakely ignored Mick's attempt at hospitality and spoke to his chauffeur. "Wait outside," he said. "This should not take long."

After the chauffeur had gone, Blakely gave Mick an intense look then sat in the straight backed wooden chair beside the desk.

"You appear distressed by my visit," he said, "and your analytical mind is no doubt searching for the reason behind it." From behind hooded lids, he swept the room with a disdainful glance and he sniffed, as if offended by his surroundings. "It's quite apparent that your business has been slow, but perhaps I can stir things up and get you back on track. Reliable sources have informed me that you are a man who can keep his mouth shut and successfully dig into old secrets to ferret out the truth. I am willing to gamble—that might not be a wise word to use, but I will overlook the unwise decisions you have made in the past. I will place my trust in your reputation. I want to hire you for a very sensitive job. I have always believed in viewing matters in their true light and have never spent valuable time on wishful thinking. Now there is a part of me that craves to believe in dreams, places where magic exists and everything that has happened in the past is revealed. Mr. Carver, I want you to into the facts surrounding my daughter's disappearance. Someone took my darling girl and I think it's time to find the person responsible."

Mick gazed thoughtfully at his guest, unsure how to respond. "I think I know where you're headed, Mr. Blakely," he said, managing to avoid a stammer. "I've read everything I could about your daughter's disappearance twenty years ago."

Blakely's face glowed with a satisfied smile. "And that is why I have come to you. My informant told me about your interest in cold cases. I will pay your customary fees and if you uncover anything useful, I will gladly add a generous bonus. Will you take the case, Mr. Carver?"

Mick nodded calmly even as his mind sifted through doubts. Why had Blakely chosen him, and why should a request from one of the world's richest men make him uneasy? Finally he said, "Before your expectations run wild, I want you to know that working cold cases is a hobby and I have never actually solved a case. Oh, I have turned up facts on a few cases and given information to the police, but let's put it this way, the police have never contacted me."

Blakely gave him a hard look. "I trust you to do what you think best, Mr. Carver."

Before Mick could say more, Blakely had stood up to leave. He had reached the door before he stopped and pulled a large wad of bills from his pocket. He handed the bills to Mick.

"This is your advance, and I have included my personal card. We will discuss your daily costs when I see you at my home tomorrow morning at nine sharp. I do not tolerate tardiness from anyone with whom I do business."

Mick held up his hand. "Hey, if I'm going to work this case, I don't need you to have an attitude. I'll need the names of friends, relatives, everyone you do business with, and the identity of all your servants at the time of your daughter's disappearance."

Blakely glowered and left without speaking. Mick placed the money on his desk and carefully examined the green pile. The image of his favorite casino flashed briefly through his mind but was supplanted by Blakely's weird request. He could earn a decent sum of money if he could solve this one.

―――

By early afternoon, Mick was settled in studying the micro fiche at the downtown library. It had been years since he had examined the media's take on the infamous Melody Blakely kidnapping and now a detail he had missed before was making him rethink the case. Although the FBI had investigated Melody's disappearance, they had pulled out when they failed to establish that a true kidnapping had occurred. No ransom demands had ever been made, and Blakely had unaccountably called off all official involvement after a month of disappointing results.

Added to Blakely's odd reaction, Mick noted that the man had never used the word "kidnap." He had always declared his daughter had been "taken." The conflicting use of words deserved closed scrutiny and Mick planned to confront Blakely in the morning.

The major obstacle in the case was the victim's age. Melody Blakely was only six when she vanished and it was nigh impossible to locate a victim who had been too young to generate some form of legal ID. Mick returned the micro fiche and left the library.

———

Recalling Blakely's admonition to be on time, Mick plowed through the sluggish traffic on Arden Way the next morning, passing the prestigious streets of the Arden Oaks and Arden Park Vista neighborhoods. As the country club slipped by, he came to the Blakely estate, the address almost hidden by climbing vines covering the large stone walls. He had no time to speculate on how he would get through the huge black gates because they parted the moment his tires touched the entry pavement.

Mick parked his Honda Civic beneath a stunning porte-cochere and was promptly greeted by a middle aged man he assumed was a butler. Once inside, the man immediately led Mick down a hall off the entrance.

"Excuse me," a mocking voice called out from behind them.

Mick's guide stopped and stood still, his back to the voice that had halted him, his face red. Mick glanced back to see the owner of the sultry voice and found an attractive woman gliding towards them. He at once recognized Sonata Blakely from the many years the social columns had followed her reckless escapades. Though she had lost the vibrancy of youth, she had retained a fine patina of her past beauty.

Sonata sidled up to Mick, smoke from a burning cigarillo forming a cloud around her feathered hairdo like a halo. She sized him up but quickly became bored. "Hmm," she said. "Father said to expect you. His money is again burning a hole in his pocket, all because he refuses to let go of the past."

Mick exchanged a brief probing glance with her shining brown eyes and wondered what the drug of choice was for the day. "Since you seem to know why I'm here," he said, "I'd like very much to speak with you before I leave."

She spun around as though the floor was made of glass. "Franklin will know where to find me," she muttered. Mick gave her a final glance before turning to follow Franklin. It was obvious the woman was doped to the gills and he wondered if the wealthy patron knew what was going on under his roof.

Franklin guided Mick to an massive and intimidating carved wooden door and wordlessly left him. Mick gripped the brass knob and entered a room that had been seen in so many movies that it now appeared both familiar and antiquated. Books lined the shelves of three floor to ceiling mahogany bookcases. The obligatory world globe fit nicely alongside a bar built of marble. The expected final ingredient of the collage sat unsmiling behind a large plain desk, his gray eyes alert, his face displaying his annoyance.

Blakely pulled an old fashioned watch from the fob pocket of his vest and said, "You are five minutes late, but I have no time or inclination to tackle the issue." He nodded towards a carton on the corner of the desk. "I have gathered all the materials you requested. Please be gentle with the photographs. Many are irreplaceable, especially those of Melody. I have made notes of friends, acquaintances who have died, and done my best to resurrect what information remains concerning the servants. And my son, Dillard, has agreed to spare you some time."

Mick drew a blank. "Ah, yes, your son," he said, covering up. Why hadn't he heard about the scion of such a wealthy man?

"Don't snow me," Blakely snapped. "You aren't the first person who has either forgotten or never known about Dillard. He was born during my first marriage and is a decade older than the girls. To further confuse matters, he uses his mother's name, Agnew. I'm grooming him to take over the business. I think he has a bright future."

Mick nodded while he tried to place the brother into the equation. He said, "Want to tell me why you never verbally expressed that Melody had been kidnapped? You always speak of her as if she was plucked from the sidewalk by some harmless kook. It's almost as if you haven't accepted her loss."

Blakely threw his arms up, obviously annoyed. "Why should my choice of words matter? After her mother passed, Melody became the light of my life. Now I understand it was probably because she looked so much like my beloved wife she could have been her clone. It has been soothing to think that she was snatched by someone without evil intentions. It is foolish, but I like to think she was taken because she was like a budding rose and someone wanted to have some beauty in his or her life.

33

Mick hoped Blakely had not seen the incredulous expression on his face before he lowered his head. He was sure Blakely's emotional display had not been done to garner sympathy, but he could pity the man who had or could possess everything he wanted.

"Any place I can go through these papers?" Mick asked.

Blakely rose from his seat. "Feel free to use my desk," he said. "Stanford, my secretary, will settle the matter of your daily fee. Take your time. I must go now." He quickly strode from the room.

Mick dumped the contents of the box on the immaculate desk and then sat in Blakely's leather chair. He wondered if money was really the root of all evil, why no one had ever demanded a ransom for Melody. If she had not been taken for money, then why had she been taken? Had one of Blakely's business foes sought revenge by breaking the guy's heart? He pulled the pictures out and place them to the side so he could organize the papers and with luck uncover an overlooked detail that would lead to something significant. And there it was. One crucial fact that Blakely had without doubt hidden from the news and police. But why expose it now? Mick read every word of the medical report from the fancy mental hospital in Sutter County. Now he could see why Sonata's life had derailed. How could she be "normal" after attempting to drown her sister when she herself was only six years old?

———

After another hour, Mick dumped everything back into the box, except the photos. Only a few hours on the case and already he felt emotionally drained. He stared at a photo data May 12,

1987. Melody was engaged in some kind of game with Sonata and there was Dillard in the background. The son he never knew existed. Mick added the pictures to the box and left the room.

Franklin waited just outside the door, and he was talking.

"Ms. Sonata wants you to come to the recreation room, sir. It's just down the hall."

Mick thanked him and proceeded down the hall. He smelled the marijuana before he reached the room and was astonished that Sonata was so open with her vices. He opened the door silently and immediately wished he had announced his arrival in some way. Dillard held Sonata in a close embrace, his hands roaming in forbidden terrain. Sonata's throaty moans indicated they had been at this for some time. Mick hesitated and wondered if he should step back into the hall and clear his throat to warn them of his presence. The decision was snatched from him when Sonata turned her head and speared him with a sensuous glance. Mick did not want to believe that they had no shame for their actions and he coughed to cover his embarrassment.

Sonata glided across the room leaving Dillard with a disappointed but defiant smirk on his face. "Oops," she said to Mick. "I didn't mean for you to see that."

"Yeah," Mick agreed, "and the world isn't round. Look, I'm not here to judge your moral values. I just want to know what you recall of the day Melody vanished."

Sonata rolled her eyes and pouted. "Are you mad or what? I was only eight years old."

"You were only six when you tried to drown her."

Dillard moved fast but Mick was faster. He not only blocked Dillard's blow but delivered a short chop to the man's abdomen. Mick caught his breath and said, "It seems you're quite protective of Sonata. How did you get along with Melody?"

Dillard, clutching his abdomen, suddenly exploded with braying laughter. Mick glared at him until he realized Dillard was actually foaming at the mouth.

"Care for that spoiled brat?" Dillard sneered. "She was always ruining things for Sonata. She got the biggest gifts and the finest clothes just because the old man thought she looked like her mother. What a farce. I made her disappear all right, right under their noses. The FBI isn't all it's cracked up to be, you know."

Mick was breathing hard. A confession and he had no way to corroborate it. Mick knew he had to keep him talking. Blakely deserved to know what had happened to his daughter. "You must have been proud to outwit them," he said, "but how did you dispose of the body?"

Dillard sloshed a drink over himself before he could get it to his mouth. Angry, he threw the glass across the room. It shattered against the stone fireplace and the harsh sound stirred Sonata from her drug-induced lethargy. She darted an angry look at Dillard. Her words were slurred as she shouted, "Shut up, you drunken fool. This worn out dick doesn't know anything. Let's keep it that way."

Mick ignored Sonata, hoping to convey a sense of collusion with Dillard. "So how did you outsmart everyone?" he asked.

"My plan was ingenuity personified," Dillard returned, his voice escalating as though he could not wait to expose his secrets. "Father has always said I have potential, though I know he despises me. The fool could never imagine in a thousand years where his 'angel' is resting." He broke off to cackle inanely and pointed at Sonata. "I did it for her. I love her, but what future is there for us, a pair of star-crossed lovers, eh?"

Mick prodded. "What did you do with Melody's body?"

"Why, she's resting in her mother's arms. Where else would a young girl be?"

One minute the room was eerily quiet as Dillard made his horrible disclosure then Blakely flew in to the room, his face livid. He held a .45 automatic in one hand and he grabbed Dillard with the other. "I've waited so many years to hear you confess, boy," he said. "I've always suspected you. Oh, yes, I knew about you and Sonata. Why do you think it's been so easy to find drug dealers around? I paid them to see that you always had a good supply and I've laughed to myself as I watched you both become addicted and your lives dwindle down to nothing. But I've waited long enough to hear the truth from your bastardly mouth and you have obliged."

Spittle flew from Blakely's mouth but as the duplicity of his words sank in, Mick roared with anger.

"You played me good, old man, and now I want to know more. Your story was a fake from the start. Tell me why you called Dillard a bastard."

Blakely kept his eyes glued on Dillard and spoke without emotion. "His mother was a tramp. The timing of his birth proved I couldn't be the father. But after our divorce, she begged me to care for her son and I obliged out of some false sense of duty." His eyes darkened and he tightened his grip on the gun. "If I had known what a viper I sheltered under my roof, I would have killed him long ago"

Having heard enough, Mick lunged for the gun. The mogul, his strength magnified by anger, struggled until the gun exploded. Only then did Blakely come to his senses. He stared at Dillard's bleeding body spread before his feet and his eyes held nothing but hate.

————

Mick settled into a small office in a strip mall near Mack Road in south Sacramento. After six months of drumming up business, he could not complain. It was surprising how many people required his services to clarify the legal jargon on confusing documents. Jealous, outraged clients clogged his office asking him to get the low down on cheating spouses. Life was good, and Mick occasionally visited the gaming tables.

When the story broke about Maynard Blakely's son losing his life in a shootout with a burglar, Mick wagged his head. It seemed he had been right all along. Money could buy almost everything. Unfortunately for Sonata, money could not keep her away from drugs and she had walked that dark path to rehab too many times before. As for Blakely, he took a long vacation though some observers swore he lost his mind after his son was killed. Maybe that was why he disinterred his wife from her grave and held a strange ceremony. Even his closest friends speculated why there were two caskets in the service.

Mick accepted the huge sum of money Blakely willingly shelled out. The money allowed him infrequent visits to the casinos. But despite his attempts to forget his part in Blakely's day of retribution, he knew the memory would stay with him. The devil was always owed his due.

In the Pocket of a Dead Man

SM Caruthers

PRELUDE

"Get out, old man, and give me that cell phone. I need to call in a loan." Ben Hadean pushed the old man reeking with body odor out of the back seat of the van.

"I just wanted a ride to my sister's place," the old man argued. "She's gonna help me with the green for my next, you know— Please take me all the way up the hill. I got the address right here."

"We aren't putting up with that fucking dog anymore, old man. She's whining and pissing up my car." The three men in their mid-twenties eyed the sheltie pup still on the back seat of the black van and pushed her out, too, leaving the old man and the dog standing beside the two-lane road in the Santa Cruz Mountains. The man's hiking pants seemed incongruous on the rainy November evening. The silvery, dark brown hair of his beard wavered in the wind. Icy night put her fingers out and the Middle-Eastern passenger slid the door shut, laughing. The van pulled away.

The old man looked up at the moon between the clouds, picked up a heavy stick he found protruding from the brambles and whistled to the dog. The William Tell Overture. The old man smiled, glanced at an address on an envelope and thrust the envelope back into his pocket.

A pathway through a winter brace of vines appeared as the old man and puppy moved up the hill. A nearby mailbox indicated that the address was not far. The old man followed the path, stopped a moment and unzipped his shorts. As he finished his business, he heard a sharp snapping sound and felt a penetrating pain in his calf and chest. Gasping in shock on the damp, icy ground, the last thing he smelled before he died was the warm breath of the young dog, Queen.

———

It was Thanksgiving. Everyone was gathering at the Marr household for dinner. Alexa answered the door thinking the bell meant another guest arriving. Instead Deputy Garson stood under the icy overhang, waiting to ask questions.

"Just routine, ma'am," the deputy said.

Alexa hesitated, then asked him in, closing the heavy door behind him. She touched the tip of her nose, making one of her habitual thinking gestures.

"Would you like some coffee, Deputy Garson?" she asked.

"Well, yes, ma'am, that'd be welcome."

"My office is just past the kitchen, sir. You can wait in there. I'll get that coffee." Alexa pointed to her room as she gathered a mug and teaspoon. "We're having a family dinner, so I hope this won't take long."

The man sat in an easy chair. Across the end table, in a papasan chair, a Siamese cat lay asleep on a dark rose cushion. Alexa came in with two steaming mugs, handed one to the officer and kept the other. She leaned her butt against the computer desk. Her hazel eyes seemed to penetrate the officer's head as she said, "Please go ahead with your questions."

"Well, ma'am, we found a homeless man froze down near Highway 17, and the only identification on him was this envelope with your address on it as a return address. There weren't no letter inside. But the envelope is real old and it's written to a Colonel Ronald Phillips in the Air Force in Vietnam. The canceled postmark says 1970. Do you know of anybody with that name? He had a young dog with him, if that helps you identify him."

"I don't know anybody with that name but my mother or brother might. Excuse me a moment and I'll check. Finish your coffee, sir." As Alexa walked by, she opened the oven. She looked at the meat thermometer in the turkey as she pondered the news. How did she inquire politely after a dead man at her family's homecoming? She ran her fingers through her short brown curly hair and sighed. Puzzles came in different sizes and at odd times. Usually she responded with all her wits.

In the living room, her mother, Mary, stood talking to her son, Alexa's brother, Raymond, about the family tree farm. She was praising her foreman, Lorenzo. Raymond's wife, Tara, sat in a low chair next to her two children, who were playing scrabble. Great Aunt Pat sketched the game players as she sat near the fireplace. Aunt Pat was 85 and a retired magazine illustrator.

Alexa commanded their attention. "Deputy Garson is in my office," she said. "He wants to know if anyone here knows a Colonel Ronald Phillips."

Mary gasped and sat down on the floral patterned couch. "He's dead, MIA," she said. "He's been dead for over 20 years. He died in Vietnam."

"But, Mother, who is he and why would someone from our house be writing to him in Vietnam?"

Everyone turned toward Mary.

"He is, or he was my half-brother, a much younger brother. He joined the Air Force in the mid 1960s in defiance of my parents' wishes. But he kept up a correspondence with me. I didn't tell you about him because of the strife with your grandparents. You and Raymond were little when Ronald went missing in 1970. What could the deputy possibly want with him now? Did they find his body in Vietnam and want a family member to take care of the burial?"

Alexa put up her hand in a quieting gesture. "No, Mom, it's something quite different. The deputy found an old envelope with his name and our address on it in the pocket of a tramp, a dead tramp. I'll tell Deputy Garson that you know Ronald Phillips, and we will see what develops. Okay?"

Mary sat on the couch, her wrinkled right hand squeezing a decorative glass ball, her son beside her, obviously stunned. Alexa returned to her office with the information that the dead man might be her uncle and asked Deputy Garson to follow her to the living room.

The Deputy entered the room and said, "Mrs. Marr, we'll need you to identify the body. Alexa can accompany you."

"I'll be contacting Colonel Benson, my ex-husband, who's a member of Army Intelligence to see if he can track down our mysterious uncle's past," Alexa said as she and her mother put on warm coats.

Later, she patted her mother's arm reassuringly and then held her close as they viewed the dead man at the coroner's office.

"I'm certain this is my brother, Ronald," Mary said with tears in her eyes. She had had no idea he was alive and in the United States. "Though he never wore a beard at home, it's the scar above the eyebrow from a childhood bicycle accident that makes me certain."

"Air Force records can confirm the identity," Alexa said.

As for the young Sheltie dog, it would have to be quarantined as a possible source for the two puncture wounds on the dead man's skinny shanks. The medical examiner would determine the cause of death, but it looked like murder to the sheriff, if the dog hadn't bitten the tramp.

The two women returned home to a very different kind of Thanksgiving. Mary told her family that her mother and stepfather had not wanted to speak of Ronald. In their deep sorrow, they wanted her to keep his MIA status a family secret. Mary had hidden most of the older family photo albums.

"You probably saw pictures of Ronald in a few of our photo albums," she said, "and didn't connect him with your Uncle Bob and me, since he looked more like the Phillips' side of the family and not my mother's. He had a dark complexion and wavy black hair; Bob and I are blondes. When Grandma Aurora and Grandpa Adam died so close to each other in 1990, I thought why open old wounds. I didn't really think about your needs for the family history. I'm sorry, Raymond and Alexa. I honestly wish Ronald had tried to get in touch with me sooner. I missed him."

Mary started to cry, softly. Alexa put her arms around her mother and steered her to the bedroom.

"Lie down for awhile and we'll fix dinner. You must eat. Aunt Pat will call you when dinner is ready. Raymond and Tara will help and they'll all go home early today."

Alexa paged Colonel Mallory Benson later that evening. Though divorced, they had remained close friends, and both were good at analyzing problems. Alexa solved problems for businesses in the Bay Area as a regular part of her computer consulting company, along with helping her mom run the family farm. She was an amateur sleuth; she had sent a house burglar to prison with her fast sketch of him just a few months ago. It looked like her business might be expanding to crime solutions on the side.

Alexa met Mallory on Sunday at the Starbucks near Justin Hermann Plaza in San Francisco. Mallory was deep in the *Sunday Punch* when she arrived.

"Wouldn't you know it," he said, opening an overstuffed file folder, "she's brought her database."

"I hope it will be full of data, soon," Alexa volleyed back.

"Okay, here it is," Mallory said, "sweet and simple. Lt. Ronald Phillips came out of Vietnam in 1973 in a 'crazy' frame of mind, with an anti-war attitude. After an honorable discharge, he joined the ranks of longhaired students at Washington State University and finished a Ph.D. in Physics. Apparently, he never went home again nor told his parents that he was back in the US of A. Instead he merged with the hippie community on an island in Puget Sound, turning into an alcoholic and hermit. He disappeared around the time of Desert

46

Storm in 1991-92. He reappeared in San Francisco in 1995 clean-shaven. With his Air Force credentials, he became a professor at San Francisco State from the fall of 1995 until last spring. He was supposed to be on sabbatical this fall doing research on a physics treatise.

"That's about all we have on him. He seems to have overcome his psychoses and integrated himself back into the community. Your family should certainly be proud of him. I have no idea what he was doing, filthy and dying with a dog beside him near Highway 17. It doesn't fit the current picture of this man."

Mallory reached out for Alexa's hand. "I'm sorry," he said, "that your mother lost her brother before he found her again. Let me know if I can help or if you want a proper military burial."

Alexa licked her lips and choked on the feelings that the description of her lost uncle brought. She managed to say, "Thank you, Mallory, we'll call you." Then she closed her laptop while Mallory gathered up the *Chronicle*, tucking the Pink entertainment section under his arm and leaving the rest of the paper on the spare table.

On Monday morning, Alexa arrived at the medical examiner's office in San Jose. Deputy Coroner Martin Olmstead had already received faxed copies of the military dental records stating that the homeless tramp found beside Redwood Estates Road and Highway 17 was Professor Ronald Phillips, a.k.a. Air Force Lt. Ronald Phillips. The ME's office had found that Professor Phillips had died from a heart attack caused by some toxic quantity introduced into the body through the two punctures on his leg, but as yet they did not know what the toxic potion was or what had caused the punctures, only that they were not from the dog.

Alexa took the 6 month old puppy to Raymond's house in Los Gatos where his children welcomed her.

"She is a duty they'll love," Tara said.

Alexa borrowed their phone and called San Francisco State University implying that she was considering hiring Ronald Phillips as a consultant for one of her firm's computer projects. The physics department secretary referred her to the department head, Dr. Avran Eskald. She set up a meeting the next afternoon at 2 p.m. on campus in the faculty lounge.

Dr. Eskald was accommodating and told Alexa that her uncle was competent and clean cut and an advisor to a student group. Professor Phillips had been asked by some of the Ethiopian, Saudi and Lebanese students to sponsor their study group, which needed to network with people from their own cultures. Dr. Eskald provided the names of some of these students. Alexa promised to notify them and Dr. Eskald of the memorial service. Dr. Eskald led her into Professor Phillips office and left.

In looking through the office, Alexa found a military photo of her uncle and a small metal trunk wrapped in paper with a military return address on the floor behind his desk. Inside the trunk were letters from her grandparents and her mother, Vietnam photos and personal documents. Alexa looked at the cancellation date on the wrappings; it was from the day before the Thanksgiving holiday. She was writing a note explaining that she was removing the small trunk and its contents when there was a knock on the door and a face peered in the doorway.

"Oh, I thought you were Professor Phillips," a young olive-skinned woman said.

"Come in," Alexa said. "I'm Professor Phillips' niece. Are you one of his students?"

"Yes, he was tutoring me and I wondered if he missed our session because of illness or absentmindedness," she smiled ruefully. "He is sometimes distracted, but then so am I occasionally."

"Sit down. What is your name, please?"

"I am Brendena Selassi a third year student from Lebanon and Kansas. My father is Lebanese, my mother's American."

"I have some unhappy news, Miss Selassi. Professor Phillips died a few days ago."

"Oh," Brendena said, "I hope those drug dealers did not find him. I cannot bear it if they caused his death. He promised me it would go okay."

"Tell me what he was involved in, Miss Selassi. I cannot believe an uncle of mine would traffic in drugs!"

"I—I was in love with a student, a very bad man last year. He brought in drugs from the Middle East and wanted me to be a runner. He thought I was under his control. Professor Phillips got me into a student rehab group. He saved my life. My family would be very grateful if they knew. This man was a part of our study group for a short while so Professor Phillips knew of him. I hope he did not get the Professor killed." Brendena looked down at her Gap jeans and ran her fingers nervously along her arm.

Alexa looked straight at the young wide-eyed woman. "I hope the drug dealer was not the cause of his death either. But he was my uncle. I will find out. Thank you for your help. What is the name of that dealer? I have connections with the DEA and FBI. I can check out known dealers and their movements. It might absolve you of any guilt about the Professor's death. We'll have a service for Dr. Phillips in Santa Clara. Now please write the dealer's name and your address."

Brendena tore off a sheet from one of her notebooks and wrote the name Ben Hadean, then her own name, phone number and address on 19th Ave. She left after getting permission to inform the rest of her study group about Professor Phillips' death.

On her arrival home, Alexa delivered the small trunk to her mother. Then she took off for a run down through the tree farm to the edge of the hilly property. As she ran, she noticed some encroaching poison oak close to the house. She made a mental note to instruct Lorenzo to have it removed. While she and Raymond were totally immune to its touch, her mother was highly allergic. Alexa decided as she ran that Mallory could check with the DEA on Ben Hadean to see what connection he might have with her uncle. Her long stride took her back up the hill to her home clinging to the mountainside.

She did not like to intrude upon her mother's reflective mood, but she entered her mother's room after her run. A photo of Lt. Colonel Ronald Phillips was on the dresser among other family photos. Mary held an open album in her lap as she stared out the huge bay window.

"Mother, did you find any clues in the little trunk?" Alexa asked.

"No, just reminders of what a good mind he had and how sensitive to right and wrong he was. I had no idea he was alive. He must have just gotten our address after all these years. At least, the date on the wrappings indicates that. He never visited here. Do you think we can find out more about him at his campus office and in his apartment? I want to understand what happened."

"Of course, Mother. We'll see if the key to his apartment is in his effects. He didn't have a wallet, you know. I'm going to check with Mallory about his movements in these last few days. I'll be in my room if you need me."

Alexa's room had a large computer desk, a PC and bookshelves on two walls. It also had a magnificent view of the Santa Cruz Mountains. A hazy vision of the Santa Clara Valley appeared in the distance with Lexington Reservoir below. She felt the clarity of this view allowed her to resolve her thoughts.

"I suppose my inner vision works like the Condor in his glide across the mountain, seeking clues," she reflected. "While I am seeking clues to find out about my uncle's death, the Condor looks for dinner hints." Alexa smiled then she called her mother's doctor for some medicines to calm her and asked about one other item that occurred to her.

She emailed Mallory, asking him to fax her information from the DEA about Ben Hadean and his associates. As Alexa listened to the oldies station on the radio, the puzzle fell into place, at least an important piece did. "Poison ivvvy," the voice wailed as Alexa shut off the radio and retrieved her phone from her desk.

She called Deputy Coroner Olmstead and asked him to do a bit of research, which he readily agreed might help the Medical Examiner's investigation. By then, her fax machine was humming.

She snatched the papers up and exclaimed, "You've come through again, Mallory!" It was December 8 and time for an early gift for her family.

On that windy, rainy afternoon, an odd congregation of souls gathered at the Marr home. In addition to Alexa and her mother, the gathering included her brother Raymond, his wife Tara, Mallory, Deputies Garson and Olmstead, and Brendena.

Alexa sat in the big-armed chair by the lit fireplace and rubbed the puppy's head. Alexa told her story and put the last pieces of the puzzle together.

"Professor Ronald Phillips," she said, "was a kind man who saw a wrongful act, someone ruining a life, yours, Brendena. He helped you get your act together. But that wasn't enough for him. He contacted an old buddy from his war days connected to the DEA. He volunteered to go undercover to get information that would stop the dealer, Ben Hadean, from importing heroin from the Middle East. As Professor Phillips found out, foreign students at San Francisco State were a prime opportunity because of their normal travels back and forth to their countries to visit relatives. He allowed drug people see him degenerate into an alcoholic and a psychotic state. He made a regular heroin connection with Ben Hadean and his associates. Mallory, here, discovered this information for me from a recent DEA arrest report.

"Professor Phillips relayed the vital dates and times for the big drug connection to his DEA buddy via a cell phone on the night before Thanksgiving. Ben Hadean, when threatened with a murder charge, revealed that he and two of his friends dropped Professor Phillips off that evening on the way to the heroin exchange. They were arrogant and took the cell phone as payment for the ride. But they insisted Professor Phillips was alive; he was just looking to hit up his long lost 'sister' for money for the next buy. Of course, Deputy Olmstead can testify that Professor Phillips had no needle tracks on him anywhere and his system did not contain any known drugs."

"Yes, ma'am, I'm happy to say I can testify to that fact. Professor Phillips was clean."

"I went back to the site where my Uncle Ronald was found and looked at the plant and animal life for anything that would give a clue to his two punctures. Queen did not make them. By the way, thank you, Brendena, for telling us the dog's name. No snake had caused such large wounds and it wasn't needle tracks. I did, however, see some low lying, thick vines broken off at about calf level.

"I recalled what had happened to my mother, Mary, when my father died. When she went for a solitary walk, she wiped tears from her eyes after she'd accidentally touched poison oak and had an immediate reaction. Her whole head got swollen. She was very allergic to poison oak. I checked with her doctor and he said it was very possibly a genetic disposition. Then Deputy Coroner Olmstead reexamined Uncle Ronald and concluded that he had a heart arrhythmia which in combination with a severe allergic reaction to poison oak killed him.

"If Uncle Ronald had gotten medical attention right away and cortisone shots, he might have survived, but his death was accidental and no one's fault. He was trying to get home and we should all keep that thought in mind when we remember him. He was a hero. His call to DEA put the drug dealers away."

Alexa looked up at her family with a smile in her eyes that they hadn't seen for two weeks. Christmas wouldn't be a blaze but it would be warm.

Storm Warnings

Geri Spencer Hunter

The night Herman Munson murdered his wife was the night the tornado hit destroying their trailer on Stockton Boulevard and leveling most of the trees. While the wind was blowing a hundred-plus miles an hour and lightning was turning night into day and thunder was clapping so loud it was making heads ache and ears ring, and rain was coming down in sheets and folks were running for their lives, Herman Munson, drunk as a skunk and crazy as a loon, was beating his wife to a pulp again. His beefy fist was mashing her pasty white face, breaking her beak nose and blackening her dull frightened eyes. His feet clad in heavy mud-caked boots were repeatedly kicking her frail body, fracturing her ribs leaving her gasping for air. She was valiantly trying to fight back with ineffectual slaps and pushes, to no avail. So as their tin roof sailed through the sky and their thin walls caved in and the big oak tree crashed through their picture window, her pitiful screams were swallowed up in the howling winds and her body started losing its battle with life.

Martha Munson did not deserve this awful fate. She had done nothing, not one damn thing, to justify what was happening to her. She was prim and proper, neat and tidy, seldom nagged and never talked back, a dutiful wife for thirty years, nearly as long as he'd been beating her. She washed and ironed, cooked and cleaned, endured his drunkenness and egotistical sexual pleasures. They had known each other since childhood.

Capital Crimes

They held hands in junior high, petted in high school and married after graduation. Only once did she think about leaving. If you had asked her why she stayed, she'd have said because she loved him, had always loved him, would go to her grave loving him. On this night of storm warnings and total destruction she was about to do just that.

If he had known, he might have spared her, just left her bruised and battered and half out of her mind instead of lifeless. But over all those years of togetherness, he never bothered to learn anything about her, nothing, not one damn thing. He was too busy demanding and criticizing and drinking and abusing. He took her trust, her loyalty, even her love for granted. After all, she was only his wife, his property. He could do with her as he pleased. And being the sorry creature he was, he pleased to abuse her. So, after the pounding while the wind still howled and the lightning still flashed and the thunder still clapped and folks were still running for their lives, Herman Munson committed his final unmanly act. He aimed his gun and shot his wife right in the middle of her bony sunken chest and walked away without a backward glance.

———

The whole town was in chaos. Tornadoes were a rare occurrence. The sheriff, the fire department, the health department, emergency services and all their volunteers were totally overwhelmed. Because of the panic, the massive destruction, the lingering storm warnings, the causalities, and yes, some incompetence, Martha Munson wasn't discovered for a while and when she was, nobody was particularly suspicious. Hell, a tornado had ripped the town apart. Finding a bruised and battered, even dead body was expected. Only later, when they started taking a second look, up close and personal, did they realize a bullet had caved in her chest instead of a tree limb.

The sheriff went looking for Herman. Everybody in town, including the sheriff, knew he was a drunk and an abuser. The sheriff couldn't count the number of times he had been called to the Munson trailer, found Martha broken and bleeding and Herman falling down drunk. In spite of that history, Herman had never spent one night in lockup. Martha always refused to press charges because, she reasoned, it wouldn't have happened if she'd kept her mouth shut. The sheriff got so pissed he threatened to quit responding to her calls. He never did. He was afraid what happened would happen.

———

He found Herman Munson amongst what was left of his old trailer, cradling a picture of his dead wife and crying like a baby. He didn't really want to disturb him, thinking he'd already been through enough, but his wife had been murdered and it was their job to find out who did it and he seemed the usual suspect.

"Sorry to disturb you, Herman," old Sheriff Watson said, chewing tobacco and spitting the juice between his stained teeth.

"You got to do what you got to do, Sheriff," Herman said, wiping his nose with the back of his hand.

"Just need to straighten out a few things."

"Go ahead."

"Where were you the night the tornado hit?"

"Drinking."

"At home?"

Herman shook his head. "No, sir, at a bar in the south end of the county."

"What's that, ten, fifteen miles down the road?"

"Fifteen to be exact."

"See the tornado?"

"I didn't see it but heard the warnings. That's why I stayed put. I wanted no part of no tornado."

"So you wasn't at the trailer during the storm?"

"No, sir, I sure wasn't."

"Didn't see Martha?"

"No, sir. I stopped by after to check on her, make sure she was all right."

"What'd you find?"

"What'd you think I found? Destruction, nothing but total destruction. She wasn't nowhere around." He started crying again, tears running down his cheeks and pooling at the corners of his mouth. "Trailer gone, wife gone. Might as well have taken me, too. I should have been around to protect her."

"How'd you find out where she was?"

"Figured she was in the shelter across town, but she wasn't and nobody remembered seeing her."

"What'd you do then?"

He swallowed his tears. "Somebody suggested checking the hospital or the . . . morgue."

"That's what you did?"

"Checked both, found her at the— Doc said a tree limb had fallen on her during the storm and crushed her chest."

"Well, that's what Doc first thought, but when he took a closer look, he found a bullet not a tree had killed her. She was murdered, Herman."

Herman's crying grew louder.

"Know anybody who'd want to kill her?"

"No, sir," he mumbled between sobs.

"You know what I'm thinking, Herman?"

Herman looked at the sheriff and shook his head.

"I thinking, maybe it was an accident. Maybe the person didn't mean to kill her." He was staring at Herman, looking him right straight in his eyes. "Maybe the person had too much to drink, you know, and Martha got to arguing and naggin, made the person mad. Hell, a man ought to be able to have a few without the naggin."

"Damn right," Herman grumbled.

"Ticked him off," Sheriff Watson continued. "He started pushin and shoven, slappin her around a bit. That what happened, Herman?"

Herman didn't respond.

"Yep, wives can sure piss you off with their fussin. Martha ever piss you off, Herman?"

"Naw, Martha was a good woman, never nagged."

"Even when you came home soused and started hittin on her?"

"Never hit her," he mumbled.

"We both know that's a lie. I made too many visits and Martha showed up at Doc's too many times."

"Okay, I hit—"

"Beat, Herman."

"Okay, I beat her. I ain't proud of that, but I sure in hell didn't kill her."

"I think you did. What I can't understand is why you shot her. Hell, with that tornado carryin on you coulda got away with beatin her to death. Hard to prove bruises and fractures weren't from walls and trees cavin on somebody. But a bullet? I just can't understand the shootin."

"Sheriff, I told you, I didn't see her and I sure in hell don't know nothing about no bullet."

"You own a gun?"

"Used to."

"What happened to it?"

"Got rid of it long time ago. I drink too much and get too crazy to have a gun around the place."

"Mm hmm."

"Anything else, Sheriff? I need to start cleaning up around here."

"Guess that's about it for now, Herman."

"Let me know what you find out."

"Oh, you can count on that. In the mean time, don't you go no where, hear?"

"I'll be right here, Sheriff. I'll be right here."

———

The night Herman Munson put his gun in his mouth and blew his head apart, the skies were clear, the winds were calm and he was stone cold sober.

The Award

R. Franklin James

Remy Pearson sat in the interview room with the shutters closed. Until today, she had always liked this room with its ultrasuede chairs, Parsons table and Stiffel lamp. Until today, she liked being a paralegal. The divorce after seven years was a setback, but overall she had come to her thirty-five years much wiser. Three of those seven years had wreaked havoc on her personal life, but she'd trimmed down to a size eight, cut her shoulder length mane to a short perky crop and ditched her glasses for Lasik surgery. She was getting back on track. Until today.

Today, she found Eric Turner, her supervising attorney, sprawled on the floor across the entrance to her office. Today, the first thought that came to her mind was if they would ever be able to get the blood out of the carpet. Today, the second thought that crossed her mind was that it was clear the gash in his head had been made with her Employee of the Year Award. The gray resin pyramid lay in the blood that pooled under his matted hair.

It didn't take long for the Oakland police to arrive and by 8 a.m. the partners, associates and admin staff had started to drift in. Everyone was directed to the main conference room to wait until called to the interview room for questioning. Remy was first. A handsome detective stood over her, notepad in hand.

"You don't seem to be too upset, Ms. Pearson," he said. "Why do you think Mr. Turner was in your office?"

"I've been assigned to him for the past eight months. And he actually wasn't "in" my office. He was in my office doorway." Remy gave him an assessing look.

"Then, why your office doorway?"

"I don't know," Remy said, more to herself than him. "He rarely came inside my office."

"Was there more between you two than just a working relationship?"

"I'm sorry, what is your name again?" she asked.

"Detective John Cadis. Now, please, answer my question."

Remy sighed and looked up at the ceiling. "No, we were just co-workers."

"Did you like him? Was he well-liked in the office?"

She hesitated. "I can't speak for the others. He was okay."

Cadis raised his eyebrow. "Hardly a resounding endorsement. Did you know his wife?"

Remy shook her head. "He wasn't married."

"Oh, but he was. She lived in the house at Tahoe while he worked here during the week."

She paused. "Nah, he couldn't have kept that a secret. This is a small law firm. He said he was divorced."

"Sorry to disappoint you. He was married. Maybe he knew you would be angry."

Remy was about to spit out a few of her favorite expletives but stopped as she noticed the piercing look the detective was giving her. It had not been too long past that she had faced that same look from a judge who had sentenced her to three years at

Chowchilla. Her adrenaline warning system kicked in. While she hadn't exactly lied on her job application, she may have skipped checking the box about criminal convictions.

"I could care less," she said carefully. "I didn't kill him."

Cadis nodded and jotted a few more notes. "Ms. Pearson, you told the officer on the scene that you hadn't touched anything since arriving. Are you absolutely sure?"

"Well, I touched the phone, and I touched Eric's wrist to check for a pulse. No, that's it."

"We didn't find any prints on the award, at all."

Remy had nothing to say to that. No one knew about her past. She had made sure.

"When was the last time you saw him alive?"

"Friday, we have—I mean, we had a big case to get out and he was still working on his drafts and—" She paused.

"What? What did you just remember?" Cadis prodded.

"Well, those aren't the clothes he had on at work. It was casual Friday, but he was wearing something else." Volunteering information—this is what had gotten her into trouble the first time.

Remy saw Cadis give his buddy a knowing look.

Cadis tucked his notebook into a jacket pocket. "Well, that's it for now. The crime scene people are still here so you won't be able to get into your office until tomorrow."

———

Eric Turner married. She could think of at least two other staffers who also hadn't known. In the conference room, the attorneys were on cell phones and conversations were buzzing.

Within seconds of her arrival, however, the sound level dropped to near whispers.

Mr. Burnell, one of the managing partners, motioned her to come forward. He was an impressively built man for one in his eighties. His eyes were sharp and his tongue sharper still. "Remy, what was Eric doing in your office? Was there hanky panky going on?"

"Mr. Burnell, really I—"

"Did he finish the Harris filings? We've got an appearance at nine tomorrow morning. He promised me he would have them on my desk by noon today." Burnell repeatedly tapped the table with his forefinger.

Remy decided to answer the last question first. "He gave me the complaint, motions and declarations, but I don't know if he had finished the points and authorities yet." She paused, noticing that everyone in the room was paying attention. "And no, there was no hanky panky going on between us."

Burnell sniffed. "Madison, you'll have to take over. Ask for a continuance. Clark is a decent judge. And you'll have to do some care and feeding of our client. I don't want them pulling their retainer." He straightened up in his chair. "And you, Remy, I'm not going to get into your personal business. Looking at Roberta's face, I can tell I must be saying something against some employment law, but this is for everyone and not just you. This is a place of work and not a dating center. Fifty-years ago, I—"

He was interrupted by Cadis opening the door.

"Mr. Burnell, would it be possible to talk to you now?"

"Yes, let's get this over with." He stood up and gingerly took steps forward. The attorneys sitting near him pushed in their chairs to make way for him to pass.

Remy took an empty chair nearest the window. Eric Turner had started with the firm about four years ago. Handsome, charismatic and brilliant, it had been a real coup for Burnell, Madison and Burnell to snare him. But he had come on to her from the beginning, tiring only after her repeated rejection.

Her nerves and thoughts went to her ex, Phillip Garnett. Good ol' Phil had never met a quick dollar scam he could turn his back on. Of course, when his latest scam of insurance fraud blew up, he had no problem turning his back on Remy. She had gotten out for good behavior after serving only half her sentence. She changed back to her maiden name. Unfortunately, she would never be able to live out her dream of becoming an attorney. You could still be a paralegal and a felon. Looking around she thought it amazing how one could feel so isolated in a room full of people.

She looked up when Jill Willows, a fellow paralegal, sat next to her. "Remy, what did the police ask you?"

Remy counted Jill as a 'friendly,' which was more than she could say for Marie and Linda, the other two paralegals in the firm.

She leaned forward so that only Jill could hear. "The usual questions, when was the last time I saw him, did I know the jerk was still married?"

Jill flinched. Remy immediately regretted her tone. Jill reminded her of a pale specter. Everything about her appeared fragile. Her flaxen blond hair, her startling clear blue eyes and her skin that was almost translucent. It was hard to believe that she had done such earthly things as getting married, birthing a darling daughter and divorcing. Marie had told her Jill had cleaned up with her settlement.

"I've never been questioned by police," Jill mumbled, pulling at the sleeves of one of what must be a closet full of oversized sweaters.

Remy nodded. "It's not much fun, but it's over fairly quickly."

Jill leaned back, engrossed in her own thoughts.

Remy's mind went to the scene this morning. Why was Eric coming to her office? He was somewhat of a snob and rarely came into the administrative side of the firm. There was another thing that bothered her. Eric wasn't wearing his Movado watch. He would flash it around at every opportunity.

A second detective opened the door and called out into the room, "Ms. Willows?" Remy patted Jill's hand as she stood.

Another hour passed and less than a half dozen employees remained. Remy got up and headed toward the law library. The receptionist looked up from her phone call and gave her a tentative smile.

"Going somewhere, Ms. Garnett?" Palmer, Cadis' sidekick, had appeared from nowhere.

Remy froze. "How did—"

"We ran prints from your office. Can we assume that your employer does not know about your conviction?"

Remy nodded her head slowly.

"We have a call in to your parole officer," Palmer said. "Can you account for your whereabouts on Sunday?"

"Former parole officer and he'll vouch for me," she said. "On Sunday, I was at home doing laundry, running errands and cleaning the refrigerator with my roommate."

"She was with you every moment?"

Remy hesitated. "No, she had to go to LA and I took her to the airport about 2 o'clock."

Palmer just looked at her.

"Wait a sec. Am I considered a suspect?"

Just then Cadis came out of the interview room. He said, "Everyone here is a suspect."

Remy stepped back. They must have GPS locators on.

Cadis folded his arms. "Ms. Garnett, I am truly impressed. I just got a rave review from your former P.O. He thinks you were framed." Cadis held up two fingers in mock quotation marks.

"He knew I was innocent." Remy gave him a small smile. "Look, Eric owned an expensive watch, but he didn't have it on when I found him."

Palmer stood next to her. "What kind of watch?"

"A Movado Museum piece."

"Are you trying to tell us that you think someone killed him for a watch?" Cadis smirked. "It's not exactly a Rolex."

Remy hoped that her face did not reflect the irritation she was feeling. She took a breath. "Is there— I mean, do you have to tell the partners about my record?"

Cadis gave her a long look then exchanged one with Palmer. "If we don't have to, we won't volunteer the fact. But I would suggest that you come clean with the firm."

Remy took another deep breath and mouthed, thank you. "Can I get my purse out of my office now?"

"If that's all, no problem. Palmer will go with you. We'll be finished with the forensics later this afternoon. You can go back into your office tomorrow morning. Just let us know if you find anything out of the ordinary."

Remy nodded. "You mean anything else."

"What?"

"I told you about the watch."

Cadis smiled. "Ms. Gar— Pearson, we made a note about the watch, but it is just as likely that Mr. Turner left it at home. We will check for it there. Besides, this was not a theft gone bad. This was definitely murder."

Her office was in perfect order except for the deep red stain on the floor and the blackish film of latent powder that rested gently on every surface possible. Palmer stood aside as she grabbed her purse and left.

———

Remy looked up at the clock. She had set up a temporary desk in the firm's library. It was already past lunch. Maybe Jill hadn't left yet. She walked the short distance to paralegal row, but Jill's office was empty. She had posted a note on her desk chair: "I'm in the file room."

Remy had turned to leave when her eyes caught the dull glare of a pyramid. There was something familiar about it. She walked over to the award and picked it up. Turning it around and taking it with her, she headed to the firm's file room.

"You did it, didn't you?" Remy asked, holding out the award.

The smile that had welcomed her faded quickly from Jill's face. "What do you mean?"

Remy shook her head. "You killed Eric."

Jill backed up into the room. "I—I thought you did it."

"Stop playing the innocent." Remy moved closer. "This award is from your office."

"Wha—What about it?" she stammered.

"It's mine."

Jill's forehead creased in confusion. She leaned against a file drawer. "How did your award get in my office?"

Remy hesitated. "That's my question. My award was the first year the firm started putting dates on them. See the date? This award on your shelf is mine. What did you do, use yours to hit Eric and grab the one out of my office to replace it?"

Jill's face was becoming increasingly red. She stood up. "Back off, Remy. I like you, but you've got this wrong."

Remy was surprised at the anger in Jill's voice, but she wouldn't back down now. "You and Eric were having an affair. Maybe he dumped you. You got angry and cold cocked him with the nearest thing handy, our four-pound award."

"If you would stop playing detective for a minute, you would realize the flaw in your reasoning," Jill said. "Eric sent me on my way two months ago. It hurt then, but not now."

Looking at angelic Jill, Remy couldn't figure if two months were long enough to get over someone. She bit her bottom lip in thought. But if not Jill, then who? She was pretty sure that once she told the police that her award was in Jill's office, she would be taken off the suspect list, only to be replaced by Jill.

"Remy, I didn't do it." Jill's voice held undeniable begging. "I don't know how your award got in my office. I haven't paid any attention to that thing since I got it."

Remy was skeptical, but ever since discovering Phil's double dealing, nothing surprised her. "I've got to tell the police."

"Can't you just wait a couple of days? Ashley is going to spend two weeks with my mother in Roseville. I can't take the time to work this out. On Thursday, I'll go with you to the police." Jill was begging now. "Remy, I swear to you I didn't do it. Besides I know—"

"What are you two jabbering about in here?" Clyde Gibbs, the firm's newest associate joined them. "Sounds serious."

"It isn't." Remy gave him a slight smile, feeling Jill's eyes on her. "Just girl stuff."

"Well, I could use some help with a pleading." He handed over a bulky blue legal file. "Jill, are you available to do the citations? Remy, I know you've got this other thing to deal with."

"Sure, Clyde, I can help you," Jill responded, still not taking her eyes off of Remy.

Remy nodded slightly. "Yeah, I got this other . . . thing. See you later, Jill. I've got to get going on some research."

Clyde was still blocking the door. He moved back to let her by. "I'm sorry about all of this, Remy. But the old man said to collect the Harris files out of your office as soon as the police finish."

"Well, that's just-just wonderful," Remy said. She looked pointedly at Jill, who was now staring at an open file perched on the shelf.

Clyde raised his arms in a calming gesture. "Yeah, I know, I know. Look, I've got to make a few calls. Jill, let me know when you've got that citation summary finished."

He breezed out.

Jill's clear blue eyes swelled with tears. "Okay, all right, forget Thursday. Just give me until tomorrow after work. I'll go to the police."

Remy nodded. "Well, I've got to get going."

"Where are you going?"

"I've got another idea about who killed Eric. If you didn't do it, then it has to be someone who had a possible reason, as well as access to the offices."

"Who?"

Remy gave her a smile and a mock salute as she went out the door.

Who indeed, Remy murmured to herself as she went back into her temporary office in the firm's law library. She had sounded a lot more confident than she felt. With her criminal record, she was an easy target. Still, she felt that there was something she was forgetting. Something someone had said today that set off distant bells.

———

The faint smell of lavender floated out from Marie's office, the air freshened by atomizers disguised as candles. Marie took her glasses off the top of her blond head and pushed them up the bridge of her nose. She peered over the rims up at Remy.

"What's up?"

"The police think I killed Eric." Remy sat down in the chair in front of her desk.

"You work for one of the best criminal law firms in the state. We can get you off." Marie picked up a small tube of French lavender lotion and massaged her hands.

"I didn't do it," Remy said. "Aren't you the least bit upset? I remember hearing a rumor that you were Eric's latest."

Marie took her glasses off. "That is none of your business. I'm sorry about your-your situation, but Eric and I had an understanding."

"I wonder." Remy looked around the office. "Someone wanted it to look like I killed Eric with my Employee of the Year Award, but my award was switched with Jill's." She got up and walked over to the cabinet and lifted up Marie's award.

"And what does the lady bountiful say to that?" Marie asked.

"Despite his faults, it seems Eric had a habit of leaving his women peacefully. Jill doesn't know anything. But, Marie, didn't it bother you that he was two-timing you?" Remy brought the award over and sat it on the desk.

"Don't you ever get tired of playing detective?" Marie picked up the award and put it back on top of the cabinet. "There was no real commitment between us. Look, I wasn't even around this weekend. I was at a real estate seminar at the Mosconi both days."

Remy sank back in the chair. "Sorry. Your alibi is better than mine."

Marie gave her a sympathetic look. "It must be rough having a police record in your background. But like you said, he wasn't really in your office. Maybe he was going somewhere else."

Remy knew she was staring at Marie. "Who told you I had a record?"

"Jill." Marie looked smug.

Remy felt her anger rising. Before she got blindsided again, she went back to the library to think things through.

Burnell had assured her that she was still on the Harris matter, at least until Madison came up to speed. So it did not seem that the management team knew about her felony. They weren't altruistic enough not to say something. Remy ignored the staff as they came into the library and, seeing her, quickly located what they were looking for and left. Everyone thought she should go home, but she wouldn't. She thought best when she was busy with routine. After a while the pieces slowly came together.

———

Stepping into Jill's office, her eyes ran quickly over the bookshelf full of law manuals and volumes of the Code of Civil Procedures. She pressed her fingers into the space behind the books and, turning around, she lifted the files stacked neatly on top of the desk and searched the in-tray beneath. She opened the top desk drawer and reached toward the back. Knowing she had only a few moments before someone would tap on the closed door, she pulled open the file drawer and flipped quickly through the pendeflex folders. Jill, like most of the paralegals, was compulsively organized, so the folders were neat and orderly. But the black banded watch with red smears across its face, wrapped in tissue and tucked into the last file folder, was not.

———

Capital Crimes

Jill stood in front of the wall of windows in the file room with the last light of the day fading behind her. She looked like an angel, her curly hair haloed around her face, but the glare from the windows made it difficult to see her expression.

"You gave him the watch, didn't you?" Remy said.

Jill looked out the window and gave a slight sniff. "It was the first thing I bought with my alimony check. He dropped me the next week, but he continued to flash it around. I had to get it off his stinking wrist."

Remy nodded in understanding, encouraging her to go on.

Jill sat down on a file room stool. "I heard him tell one of the clerks that he was going to be working on Sunday. I just followed him in." Her expression looked pained. "I just wanted to know why he thought he could treat me this way. He was oh so patronizing. He said I should consider him a life lesson, and-and he just grinned and waved that watch in front of me."

Remy looked hard at her. "Why my award?"

Jill went on as if she hadn't heard her, her chest heaving with the memory. "I could hardly breathe. My heart was pounding so loud I thought he could hear it. He was headed to the bathroom. You know the main bathrooms aren't open on the weekend, so he had to use the ones at the end of our hallway. He turned his back to me, laughing the whole time. I knew enough to hide my fingerprints with my sleeves. I picked up my award and swung it at him as hard as I could. I wanted to bash his head in."

"But why my award, Jill?"

"Because he fell into your doorway and you've served time. I forgot that my award was different from yours. I took my watch back. I was going to clean it and try to return it to the store and—" She gave Remy a matter of fact look. "I can't go to jail, Remy. I'm the only parent Ashley has. You don't have anybody at home. I figured you wouldn't stay in jail. I just needed a little time to get things together."

"You knew about my conviction?"

"When you first got here, you missed one of your check-ins with your P.O. I accidentally picked up the call from your desk. I ran your social through DataCheck and, voila!"

Remy guessed that Jill simply thought her expendable.

"What happens now?"

Jill looked surprised. "It's over." She took a deep sigh and shook her head. "I think I'll ask Clyde to defend me. He'll come with me to the police."

Remy just nodded.

The door opened.

"You two again?" Clyde teased. "Jill, I just wanted to tell you thanks for finishing up those court docs. I owe you one."

Jill straightened her back and walked toward the door. She turned her back to Remy. "I'm glad to hear you say that, Clyde. Can I see you for a minute? I'm going to need to call on that favor."

Remy walked slowly back to the library. Putting her award at the front of the work table, she paused to give it a long look. Shaking her head, she sat down, pulled out a piece of paper and wrote: Letter of Resignation.

Playing House

Teresa Judd

Emma wondered why her new best friend wasn't in school and hadn't been for several days. Emma was a precocious five year old who delighted in being a "big girl," attending school with her very own book bag stuffed with crayons and drawings. She approached every day as an adventure. Nobody would willingly miss such a treat, she reasoned, and so at the end of the day when her mother, Jane Woodruff, had helped her into the backseat and securely strapped her into her car seat, she wasted no time in asking.

"Mommy, why isn't Sue Ann in school anymore? I asked the teacher but she didn't know."

Jane, a single mother, tried hard to give her daughter her wholehearted attention to make up for the keenly felt absence of a second parent. However, this day her mind was on the errands she had to finish before they could get home and she missed Emma's question.

"What did you say, dear?" she asked now.

"I said," Emma answered, emphasizing the word said with the long-suffering patience of a martyr, "why isn't Sue Ann in school anymore?"

"I don't know, honey. Maybe she's sick," her mother answered.

"Can we call her? I can bring her toys to make her better if she's sick."

"That's very thoughtful of you, Emma. I'll call when we get home," Jane promised. "But now we need to get you to dance practice."

After practice, they stopped off at McDonalds for takeout and by the time they got home, Sue Ann had been forgotten.

Still, the next day in class, Emma saw that Sue Ann still hadn't returned. So after consuming an after school snack of cookies and milk, she looked up at her mother and reminded her that she hadn't called Sue Ann's mother.

"You're right. I guess I just got busy," Jane said, thinking that was the understatement of the year.

Jane didn't personally know Sue Ann's mother but she had a class list so she was able to look up the number. Finding it, she picked up the phone and dialed. After listening for awhile, she put down the receiver and turned to Emma.

"They're not answering and apparently they don't have an answering machine. I'll try again later."

And she did try several times the next day but still received no answer.

When she picked Emma up after school, the first question out of her daughter's mouth was, "Did you find out about Sue Ann?"

"I'm sorry, no. No one ever answered the phone."

"Mommy, I'm afraid something bad has happened to Sue Ann. Can we go by her house?"

"Not now, honey. Let me see if I can find out where she lives. Maybe I can find out from the school."

Surprisingly, the address was listed in the phone book. Jane decided that it might be best if she checked out the situation during the day before inquiring at the school, so she drove to the house the next afternoon. Although only a few blocks away on the other side of some railroad tracks, it was a part of town that she had never visited, run down and interspersed with car repair garages and empty lots. Still, she managed to find the address despite the lack of house numbers on some of the buildings. The house was extremely neglected, in need of paint and repair. The front yard consisted of dirt, weeds and a few broken toys. The porch sagged alarmingly and Jane picked her way up to the front door with careful steps. She looked for a doorbell but finding none, knocked lightly. The house seemed quiet and deserted and despite Jane's knocking, which became increasingly louder, there was no response. She tried the doorknob and found it to be securely locked.

That day after school, she was ready with an answer when Emma again asked about Sue Ann.

"I went by the house but there was no one there. They must have moved."

"No, Mommy, Sue Ann wouldn't have moved without saying goodbye," Emma said through tears.

"She might not have had a choice. It could have been very sudden. I'll see if the school knows anything, OK?" Jane promised. She hated to see Emma so upset and knew the little girl wouldn't let it go until she had some kind of answer.

True to her word, the next day Jane approached the school administration office.

"My daughter is concerned because her friend, Sue Ann Carmody, hasn't been in school lately. Have you any information about her? Perhaps they've moved away?"

The woman behind the desk rummaged through a cabinet and pulled out a file. After looking over the paperwork, she admitted that Sue Ann had indeed been absent for a week now and there had been no notification of a move.

"It isn't too unusual for people to just leave without letting us know. Since it's kindergarten, they don't see it as important. I'll see if I can find out anything. Have you tried phoning?"

"Yes, and I even drove by the house but there was no sign of anyone."

"I see they live in a rather poor neighborhood. Maybe they were evicted."

"You'll let me know what you find out, won't you? Emma is really very upset about this."

"Of course, Mrs. Woodruff. As soon as we know something, we'll let you know," the woman said turning back to her desk.

Somehow Jane didn't think any more information would be forthcoming either now or in the future and she left the office unsure of what to do next.

That evening after dinner, Jane again drove to the house, this time with Emma safely ensconced in the back seat. The house looked the same as it had before and Jane got out of the car hesitantly. A young boy appeared around the corner, maneuvering a skateboard over the broken sidewalk with an expertise Jane envied.

"Hi," he said. "You lookin' for Sue Ann?"

"Yes. I am," Jane answered. "Do you know if they moved away?"

"I don' know, but that's their old car back there. It don't run very good, but if they moved, I think they'd have took it."

For the first time, Jane noticed the beat up Chevrolet parked towards the back of the building. That is strange, she thought. Maybe I should call the police. Still, the idea of calling in the police on such a slim suspicion bothered her so she decided to sleep on it and decide what to do the next day. She got back into the car and noted that Emma was dozing off. Just as well, she thought. Emma would probably insist that she try to get in the house. She was a very determined little girl once she set her mind to something.

The next morning Jane was still in a quandary as to what to do. She sipped her morning coffee and considered her alternatives. Take the easy way out and tell Emma that the school had found out that Sue Ann had moved away too hurriedly to say goodbye. Call the police and risk making a fool of herself over an innocent situation. Try the house one more time, maybe look around a bit.

Abruptly, she stood up and grabbed her purse and car keys. Once again, she drove to the strange neighborhood. In the morning light, everything should have seemed innocent and normal but somehow the house and surrounding yard exuded a sinister air. Jane felt as though she was being watched. Making a slow turn, she scanned the area but saw no one and heard nothing, not even the rustle of small animals or the song of birds. She tried the front door once more and got the same lack of response but this time, she walked along the side of the house, standing on tiptoes trying to see into the windows. They were all curtained or shuttered so she could see nothing inside.

With increasing foreboding, she approached the back door and knocked again. Nothing. And then she heard a slight noise inside. Probably just a rat, she thought to herself and shuddered at the sudden image of rats plural running across the floorboards.

"Sue Ann?" she called out on impulse. "Sue Ann, are you in there?"

To her surprise, the door slowly opened and a golden haired angel of about five peeked out around the door.

"Yes," she said.

"Sue Ann?"

"Yes," she repeated. "I'm not supposed to answer the door to strangers." She started closing the door again.

"I'm not a stranger," Jane said hurriedly, putting her hand out to stop the door. "I'm Emma's mom."

"Oh," Sue Ann said opening the door wider. "Then that's all right."

Behind her, Jane could see trash and dirty dishes piled on counters and a kitchen table covered with food wrappers. Dirt and crumbs littered the floor and an overwhelming smell of rotten meat wafted out. Flies circled the room lazily. Sue Ann herself looked dirty and her hands were smeared with what looked like strawberry jam."Where's your mommy?" Jane asked.

"I'm the Mommy now," Sue Ann answered.

"I see that," Jane said. "But where is your Mommy?"

"Oh. She's asleep on the couch."

"Could you go get her?"

"No. I can't wake her up. I already tried."

"Can I come in and try?" Jane asked.

"OK," Sue Ann said and opened the door for her.

Once inside the smell was so terrible, Jane grabbed a Kleenex out of her purse and held it over her nose. Fearing the worst, she walked tentatively into the darkened living room. She heard them before she saw them. Hundreds of flies. They were swarming over a body slumped on the sofa. Gagging, Jane ran from the room pulling Sue Ann after her. Using her cell phone, she called the police and then sat down on the porch with the little girl and held her sticky hand while they waited.

———

Six months later, Emma returned from her first day in the first grade and announced that Sue Ann was in her class.

Jane surmised that Child Protective Services had probably placed Sue Ann in a foster home nearby.

"That's wonderful, Emma," she told her daughter.

"And you know what?" Emma said.

"What?"

"Her new mom wants to know if we can have playdates," Emma announced proudly. Playdates sounded so much more important than just plain playing.

"Would you like that?" Jane asked, thinking of all that Sue Ann had probably had to go through. First, the death of her mother by persons unknown, which the little girl had apparently blocked from her memory. Then the impersonal housing in a county run group home. And now, a new place and new family. She would be glad to help normalize the little girl's life if she could.

"Yes. Her mom is going to call you," Emma informed her. "Sue Ann has a new last name too. It's Whitman."

"That sounds great," Jane said meaning it. The poor little girl deserves a good home, she thought.

Several days later, Marsha Whitman did indeed call.

"I was hoping you and Emma could come over for a play-date some time next week. We could have coffee while the girls play and I can tell you all about Sue Ann coming to live with us. Would Tuesday work?"

"That would be fine. Tell me where you live and what time."

When Tuesday arrived, Emma was all excited about going to her friend's house and Jane was admittedly curious about the circumstances.

The house was an upper middle class McMansion with a neatly kept yard. Marsha Whitman was a pretty woman whose looks were beginning to fade as if she had spent too much time in the shadows. But her smile of greeting animated her face with warmth, erasing any negative first impressions.

After the girls were involved in a game, Marsha and Jane sat down at the kitchen table and Marsha told Jane how thrilled she was to have Sue Ann in her life.

"Bob and I always wanted to have children but were never able to. So when we were asked if we wanted to be foster parents to Sue Ann, we jumped at the chance. She is just the sweetest little girl, very bright and cheerful. We've filed adoption papers so we registered her in school with our name to make things simpler in the future. My husband, Bob, travels a lot so it has made such a difference to have Sue Ann here."

"I know what you mean," Jane said. "I don't know what I would do without Emma. It's been hard raising her alone—I'm divorced—but she certainly livens things up." She smiled at the sound of the two little girls giggling in the other room.

After that, Jane and Marsha spent an hour or two a week comparing notes and becoming friends while Sue Ann and Emma played house. Sue Ann was always the Mommy and Emma played different roles depending on the game, the big sister, the best friend, the neighbor. Bob was noticeably absent and Marsha said he often went out of the country for two or three weeks at a time since he was in the import business.

One Monday, Emma came home and told her mother that Sue Ann wasn't in school that day.

"She probably has the flu. It's going around," Jane said. "I'll give Marsha a call tomorrow."

When Jane called Marsha the next morning she got the impersonal voice of the answering machine. Probably at the doctor's, she thought.

A couple days passed before Emma timidly brought up the subject again.

"Mommy, Sue Ann isn't back in school," she informed Jane. "You don't think something bad happened again, do you?"

"No, of course not. Still I'd better give Marsha another call," Jane said.

Picking up the phone, she dialed the number but again got the answering machine. She tried several more times leaving a message each time but did not hear back.

Stifling a feeling of alarm, Jane dropped Emma off at school and skipping a second cup of coffee, drove rapidly to Marsha's house. The house looked deserted but the car was in the driveway and even more disturbing, several days worth of newspapers were piled on the front porch.

Jane raced up to the front door and started repeatedly ringing the doorbell. Please answer, she thought.

"Marsha. Are you in there?" she called. Alarm turning to fear, she pounded on the door still calling out Marsha's name.

To her relief, she heard the lock turn inside and the door began to open.

Sue Ann stood there looking up at her.

"I'm the Mommy now," she said smiling.

Smoke Trail

Norma Lehr

When Ben, my supervisor, called me at home to inform me of Kevin Patson's death, I went into shock. "No way," I protested. "He was a young man. It hasn't been a month since I did his insurance physical. He seemed fine then." I dropped into a chair. "What happened?"

"It's been over six weeks since you examined him, Sue," Ben corrected. "And his death had nothing to do with his health. Patson died in a fire at his home. He was alone last night and probably went to sleep holding a lit cigarette. According to his wife, he was a heavy smoker.

"She's all broken up. Anyhow, I thought you'd be interested since you were here that day Cheryl Patson dropped by the office to make his appointment."

I felt sick. "How about his policy? Did it go through?"

"Yep, and it was a whopper. A half-a-mil."

Ben had called me because he thought I'd be interested. That was an understatement. When I first met Cheryl Patson I tried to place her. I knew that woman from somewhere. Her face kept flashing in my head like a pulsing strobe light, some elusive memory just out of my grasp.

I'm a paramedical examiner in Sacramento. My job is to make appointments with busy prospective life insurance clients and do routine physical exams at their home or place of business. I carry a portable EKG machine and stethoscopes and do blood pressure checks.When Cheryl Patson breezed into our office that day six weeks ago, convincing Ben that it was urgent we send someone over to her husband's office right away to complete an exam because he was taking her on a cruise for their anniversary, something in the tone of her demanding voice caught my attention. I peered around my office door and did a double take. This woman looked familiar. Ben spotted me at the door and asked me to please make room in my busy schedule for one more appointment that day.

My job is not the most exciting work on the planet, but once in a while it gets there. Like when I met Kevin Patson. Not movie star handsome but close enough. Too bad he was married. I entered his office packing my equipment and when he smiled, my heart did a little dance. But when I looked up into his blue eyes, I thought I spotted a deep sadness.

"I don't understand why my wife feels she needs more insurance," he said with a shrug as he unbuttoned his shirt. "But I suppose she knows what she's doing." He sat and inhaled deeply as I placed the stethoscope on his chest.

"Maybe she feels insecure about the cruise. According to the news, passengers have been falling overboard." I felt myself blush, wondering how I could have been so personal.

"Insecure? I don't think so. Cheryl's already well provided for." He reached across his desk for her picture and studied it. I couldn't see his expression from behind, but when I looked over his shoulder I had the feeling I knew her from somewhere, and I told him so.

"Yeah?" He turned and looked at me. "From where?'

"I'm not sure. Has she always been a redhead?"

"Always." He offered me the picture in the gold frame.

Recognition flashed in my head then quickly vanished. "Did she grow up in Ohio?"

He turned away while he shoved his arm back into the sleeve of his shirt. "Nope. Cheryl's from California. Went to Berkeley."

"That let's that out. I graduated from Ohio State." I handed him back the picture and he dusted off the frame with a corner of his shirt. "She's a real beauty, isn't she?"

"Yes," I said distractedly. "Does she have a sister?"

"Nope. Cheryl's an only child. No family. Parents are both dead."

I couldn't let it go. "Do you suppose she ever visited Ohio?"

He looked up at me with a puzzled frown. "Why the interest?"

I shrugged. "I'm not sure. She reminds me of someone I knew a long time ago."

He glanced at his Rolex. "Time for a break." He flashed that charming smile again. "How about joining me for coffee. There's a Starbucks downstairs. I don't like to drink alone."

I make it a rule not to get social with clients, and it could have been my own wishful thinking, but behind Kevin's smile I thought I sensed a loneliness. "Sure," I said, making an instant heart-felt decision. "Let's go."

Kevin's break turned into nearly an hour of conversation, with him doing most of the talking and me listening. He was intelligent and witty as he spoke of his business, golf and world affairs. At one point, he started to say something about Cheryl. There was a pause. I waited but he changed the subject.

I finished my latte and blueberry scone, excused myself and went to the ladies room. When I returned to the table, Kevin had been joined by a business associate. He introduced us and I explained that I needed to be on my way to the next appointment. Kevin handed me his business card and I could see a handwritten note on the back. I felt him staring as I buried his card in my equipment bag along with other clients cards, afraid that if I read his and he suggested we meet again, I wouldn't be able to refuse.

I felt a wave of regret when we parted, but I knew he was married. He's just another client, I told myself back in the car. Let it go, Sue.

I feel a deeper regret now that I hadn't read his jotted note. I honestly forgot about it. If I had figured out what was going on that day, I could have put my emotions aside and helped him. If I only had, he might still be alive!

After Ben's disturbing call about Kevin's death, I climbed into bed and tossed and turned for hours. Cheryl Patson told Ben he was a heavy smoker. Thinking back, Kevin hadn't lit up once when we spent that hour at Starbucks. And when I had examined him, there was no ashtray in his office and no offensive smell of cigarettes.

Around 2 a.m., I went to the kitchen for a glass of milk and spotted my equipment bag by the back door. Remembering Kevin's card, I dug through until I found it, turned it over and read what he had written.

An hour later, after searching through my bedroom closet for boxes filled with memorabilia, I finally found what I was after. Tears welled up as I imagined the horror of poor Kevin being cremated in his own bed. Burned up in a cruel fire.

I rushed to the phone, explained to Ben what I had found and asked him to help me.

He yawned an "Okay. Tomorrow. And you better have proof."

The next morning at seven, Ben came storming into the office with Earl Cancroft, the Arson Investigator from the Fire Department. Ben scowled and checked his watch. "Tell Earl what you told me last night. Don't leave out any details."

A half-hour later, after I had finished my story and shown them both the evidence I'd brought from home, Earl scratched the graying stubble on his chin and nodded. "Looks like you've got enough to get us started. The insurance company will be hitting on this soon, but why wait? Let's get this show on the road."

Ben let out a sigh of relief. Taking my arm, he guided me over to the window. "I owe you an apology, Sue. I figured your imagination was working overtime, but it looks like you're on to something."

Two days later, Ben, Earl, the sheriff, and I went to the Haven Mortuary to pay our last respects to Kevin. Cheryl Patson, dressed in mourning, stood next to the Egyptian urn resting on a polished table. I strolled over and told her I was the paramedic who had done her husband's insurance exam.

"Poor Kevin," she wailed, lifting her black veil and dabbing at her mascara. "You really didn't know him that well, did you? He was so young, so vital."

"You're right," I agreed, staring into her tearless brown eyes. "I didn't know Kevin that well. But I know who you are."

Cheryl sniffed and adjusted her veil back over her red hair. After giving me the once over, she said, "Who are you?"

"I'm Susan Goodall, a classmate of yours from Ohio State. You probably don't remember me."

Her eyelashes fluttered up in surprise. "I'm sure I don't know what you're talking about."

"And you are Candy Blackwell," I continued, "sans the blond hair and about twenty pounds." I held up the college yearbook I was carrying and opened it in front of her face. "You disappeared ten years ago after starting that fire in the dorm that killed two of your sorority sisters, the roommates who were going to turn you in for stealing from the sorority accounts. Their suspicious deaths landed in a cold case file along with a warrant for your arrest."

She stepped back, searching for an exit. "You are out of your mind."

"I think it's the other way around, Mrs. Patson," the sheriff interrupted. He moved in and took hold of her arm. "You need to come down to the office and have a little talk. You might want to call your lawyer."

Ben, Earl and I watched as he ushered her down the hallway and out into the patrol car. On our way home, Ben looked thoughtful. "I suppose Patson never suspected her, poor guy.

Never knew she was doing a number on him for the insurance payout."

It was all such a waste, I reflected bitterly while I stared out the window at the passing cars. Because of a school-girl attraction to a handsome married client, I had waited too long to take action. Ben was wrong, of course. Kevin did suspect something was amiss, but I didn't tell Ben. No point now. I removed Kevin's card from my purse and held it in my palm. Dear Kevin, I sighed, recalling how he had carefully dusted off his wife's picture frame. That's why you were so sad. You loved her. I reread his message that had led me to the pyromaniac who had murdered him.

Check your yearbooks, he had jotted on the back of his card. Let me know what you find.

Beneath Cherry Trees

Nan Mahon

Morning dew clung to scarlet cherries hanging round and ripe on the trees. The air was still cool as dawn gave light to the orchard, and most days by this time, harvesting would be well under way. But today yellow crime scene tape was stretched from tree to tree, sectioning off a square of space where the body lay.

I angled my Chevy Tracker into a ditch already crowded with police cars. Both sides of the road were lined with black and white vehicles with light racks mounted on top and San Joaquin County Sheriff painted on the doors. Uniformed deputies stood in groups of twos and threes, their thumbs hooked onto the gun belts at their waists. Two detectives, dressed in short sleeve shirts and slacks, had badges clipped on to their belts beside semiautomatics in short holsters.

"Hold it." A deputy stopped me as I climbed through the barbwire fence and tried to run past him.

"I work here."

He looked me over, eying my shorts and tank top, my sneakers.

"Not a picker," I said. "I'm an AmeriCorps volunteer."

"I don't think you want to see this."

Craning my head, I could see the body lying like a battered mannequin on the dirt in front of a row of blue portable potties. Blood soaked his shirt and jeans; his hair was matted with blood, and his face was a swollen mess of broken flesh. Bees and flies circled the body, landing on the head until someone shooed them away. I put my hand over my mouth to catch the bile that threatened to come rushing up from my stomach.

"He was beaten to death?"

"Yes, ma'am."

"Can you cover him up?'

"Not till the coroner's men get here."

Detectives crouched on their haunches and spoke softly to each other. One picked up a stick and pointed at the body. The other nodded and they looked toward the farm workers who also squatted cowboy style in the shade of a row of cherry trees. The workers wore faded jeans, soiled long sleeve western shirts and sweat stained straw hats. In a few hours the valley heat would rise near the one hundred mark as they stood on ladders and pulled fruit from the trees. Their faces and hands were tanned a deep red-brown and their skin was as hard as leather from years of working in orchards and crop fields under the summer sun.

The detective dropped his stick and stood up. "Any of you men know this guy's name?'

Not one dark eye twitched. The men sat without expression as if they had not heard.

He repeated the question in Spanish.

"Jose Lopez," an older man said.

"He part of your crew? Have family with him?"

"No family. He's just a picker."

"Where's he from?"

"I don't know," the man said. "Just his name."

At this point, the site boss, Bill Miller, came driving up. His white Ford pickup kicked a cloud of dust in the air as he slammed it to a stop in the ditch. Red faced and excited, he ducked through the barbwire fence and ran across the field to the police.

"What's going on here? You're holding up my pickers!"

The detective turned to him. "Ray Guzman, Homicide, San Joaquin County Sheriff's Department. You the foreman?"

"That's right and my people should be working right now. We're losing the morning."

"One of your people is dead."

"Oh, Jesus Christ! How long is that going to hold up this field? It's ready to harvest."

"Today. Maybe tomorrow."

"Dammit!" Bill was pulling his cell phone from his pocket.

"Don't you want to know who it is?" Detective Guzman said to Bill's back as the foreman walked a few feet away, talking on his phone.

Guzman asked more questions of the workmen, speaking in Spanish. They shook their heads and mumbled in reply. Behind the men, women and children stood watching. I spotted Angela, a five-year-old I'd been teaching the alphabet, and smiled. She waved her hand then wrapped her arm around her mother's leg. Looking closer, I noticed a large bruise on the child's arm. It hadn't been there two days ago when I brought her an ABC book. Isabel, her mother, drew Angela close and shot me a warning look when I started toward them. A single parent, Isabel took Angela to the fields with her everyday where the child played beneath the cherry trees while her mother worked.

Capital Crimes

Bill snapped his phone shut and turned to the detective. "I've got to get these workers on that bus and take them to another field. I can't lose a full day of harvest."

Guzman looked at the faces of the men and women waiting in silence. "And they can't lose a day's wages. Go on, I'll question them again tonight."

Bill began yelling in Spanish for the workers to get on the bus. "Pronto! Hurry!"

They did not hurry but moved in a quiet, orderly fashion toward an old school bus with faded yellow paint and a deep dent in the left fender. All of the bus windows were open to catch any breeze as it traveled, so a smeared layer of field dust covered the ripped seats. As soon as every man, woman and child was aboard, the driver raked the gears and the bus rolled toward another orchard. At the end of the road, the bus passed the coroner's wagon coming to the scene. Now they would cover the body and take it away to be inspected and dissected without an ounce of dignity before it was cremated or buried in some poor man's grave.

Detective Guzman went to meet the coroner's men as they climbed through the barbwire fence carrying a gurney with the wheels folded beneath it. I turned and walked to my Tracker, deciding I would head back to Stockton and the day care center where I could help some migrant children or a mother in need of assistance. I was three months into my one-year commitment with AmeriCorps and maybe my dreams of changing the world were not as realistic as I once believed. I had graduated from Berkeley with a degree in sociology and a head full of ideals. My plan was to do a year of volunteering in the field and then return to school for my master's. AmeriCorps sent me to San Joaquin County, an agricultural and dairy region in the Central Valley. It is listed as a poverty pocket in California because most of the work is low waged and seasonal. I was impressed by the beauty of the land where acres and acres of cherry orchards, vineyards, and row crops grew in the rich soil. I read that the region grossed almost two billion dollars a year and wondered why poverty was such a problem.

Maybe I was foolish at age twenty-two to think I was special enough to change anything. My mother had taught me Spanish because she was the daughter of rich Cubans who had fled their country just before a victorious Fidel Castro came rolling into Havana. After forty years, my grandparents still believed the revolution would fail and they would get their sugar plantation back one day. My mother, who came to Florida at age six, did not remember Cuba and never thought about it. Our speaking Spanish was more of a concession to her parents than anything else. Mother was a women's suit buyer for Sak's Fifth Avenue in San Francisco and my father, born in Kansas, was an executive with an insurance company based in the city's financial district. But I was determined that I was going to make a difference and help right social wrongs. How lofty it is for a child of affluence, who had only read of hard times, to believe in changing lives.

It was culture shock to find that my Cuban Spanish was different enough from what the Mexican migrants spoke that they had trouble understanding my accent. My hair is thick and dark, my eyes brown and my skin olive, but I don't believe they accepted me as a Latina. While they were polite to me, I could see they did not trust the fact that I was embracing the poverty they were running away from.

After dinner that evening, I drove to the place where the workers lived in a row of one and two room unpainted buildings and an assortment of camp trailers. Parking on the shoulder of a country road, I walked in. Shadows fell on the dirt where children played, smoke spiraled up from wobbly metal barbeques and people sat on old kitchen chairs and low porches in the cool evening, escaping the heat inside. Quiet conversation and laughter floated toward me as I approached. Someone began to strum a guitar and sing a Mexican ballad.

Detective Guzman sat with a group of men, talking and laughing. He was holding a bottle of Tecate, resting it on his crossed leg. Dressed in jeans and a T-shirt stamped with the San Joaquin County Sheriff logo, and cowboy boots, he looked like he belonged. His dark eyes watched me as I came toward him.

"Hello," I said. "You working?"

"Are you?"

Behind him, Isabel picked Angela up and retreated into one of the shacks. I started to follow, but Guzman put out his hand and grabbed my wrist. "Let it alone."

I shook myself free and walked to a group of women sitting on the stoop and sat down beside them. I had put on jeans and a shirt with sleeves because I knew the mosquitoes would be out in numbers, leaving their hatching places where the irrigation water stood around acres of grapevines and blueberry bushes.

"That was an awful sight this morning. How are the children? Los ninos?" I asked the women. "I'm sorry they saw that. Are they okay?"

Women who usually greeted me with a joke or a smile looked at the hard packed dirt and said nothing.

"Any news about how it happened or who did it?" I went on. "Don't worry, they'll catch the guy."

Two of the women got up and moved away. One picked up her child and went inside. The music stopped and mothers called to the children to come in now. A group of teen-agers lounged near a tree and watched.

I got to my feet as Guzman came toward me.

"Go on home," he said. "Let this alone."

"A man was murdered. What are you doing about it? You act like you're one of them."

"I am one of them. I grew up in places like this," he said. "My parents were farm workers and so was I."

Only a few inches taller than I, his body was muscular and hard, his short hair black and wiry. "I'm doing my job. Don't mess with things you don't know anything about."

"Just find this killer before he hurts someone else," I said with all the indignation I could muster and stalked away toward the house where Isabel lived.

The door was open and I hesitated at the threshold. Concern for Angela took me inside. The only light was from a bare bulb hanging in the middle of the room. Angela was standing near the table, stripped to her underpants, while her mother washed her with water from a pan. Isabel crooned a children's song as she touched her daughter tenderly with a wet cloth, wiping away the dirt and sticky cherry juice that clung to her body after a day playing in the orchards. I moved closer and squinted in the dim light. Purple bruises on the child's arm and stomach stood out on her brown skin.

"My God!" I said. "Who is beating this baby?"

Isabel turned and looked at me in surprise. "What are you doing here?"

"I have to report this," I said, moving away, backing into the yard.

Guzman was gone and the yard was deserted except for the teen-agers who stood watching me. I tried to look confident. Don't run, don't run, I kept repeating in my mind as I began walking toward the road where my car was parked. It was completely dark now and I stumbled on roots and rocks as I hurried toward the road. There was a killer out there and images of the battered body I saw this morning jumped into my mind. I began to run.

A hand grabbed my arm and jerked me backward. Another hand clamped over my mouth, stifling my scream. More hands pushed me against a tree and held me there. A trickle of urine ran down my leg.

Three teen-age girls stood in front of me while two boys held me against the rough bark of an oak tree. I knew the girls; just two days ago I had brought them lilac scented shampoo and new hair brushes donated from a discount store. The boys wore baggy pants, hanging low on their hips and red bandanas tied around their heads. I struggled and whimpered, but they held me there, with a hand clasped over my mouth.

"Listen," said Marta, one of the girls. "Don't scream. Just listen."

I stopped struggling and looked at her. When I gave her the hairbrush the other day, she ran it over and over through her long black hair.

"It was not Isabel who hurt Angela," she said. "You can't go to the police. Some of these people don't have no papers. We gots to take care of things ourselves and we took care of the person who hurt Angela. You're so arrogant to come here and pity us. You give us soap and feel important, like you're better than we are. Just leave this thing alone."

The boys released me and I stood trembling, praying my legs would hold me up as I inched away.

"This is a warning," Marta said.

There was moonlight on the asphalt when I reached my car. Leaning against the door, I wept. Guzman got out of his pickup and came to me, placing a hand on my shoulder.

"I was waiting for you to come out," he said.

"You let them do that," I sobbed.

"I didn't know they were going to."

"They might have killed me."

"No. I wouldn't let that happen."

"Did you know they killed that man?" I turned to face him.

"It wasn't the kids."

"But you're not going to arrest anyone."

"No. Should I arrest them all? I can't prove anything." He ran his hand through his hair. "Jose was a child molester. These people take care of their own."

"These men killed one of their own." Anger filled me at his dismissive attitude.

"Who said the men did it?"

I stared at him, considering the incredible meaning of his words. "It's still murder."

"Maybe it's justice."

At my request AmeriCorps transferred me to Sacramento and assigned me to the Hunger Commission where I worked in a huge warehouse filled with food for distribution to the needy. I finished my year of volunteer work and went back to Berkeley, changed my major, and entered law school.

Friends, family and studying keep me busy. But sometimes I picture the distrust in Marta's eyes and remember the anger in her voice when she called me arrogant. My mind flashes images of women armed with rakes, hoes, sticks, and rocks smashing the life from a man who was vile enough to commit a heinous crime against a child.

"Maybe it's justice," Detective Guzman said.

I think of little Angela playing beneath cherry trees.

Digital

Joyce Mason

There was a toe in her taco.

Bebe screamed so loudly I thought my girlfriend was having a heart attack or seizure, or maybe she had seen a mouse.

Taco turners, young girls who also knew how to roll a tight enchilada, came running from the griddle to our table at Tons o' Tacos.

Bebe kept pointing to the toe now standing upright in a pile of taco stuffing, spread out on the waxy paper along with the circle of tortilla with one big bite ripped out of it. The toe, the taco, the horror of it sat smack in the middle of the table at our booth.

I cursed, knee-jerk, when I saw what she was pointing at— and turning away from—screaming.

"Madre de Dios!"

It was gross. A big fat toe with red nail polish. A toe so ugly, you had to wonder what kind of woman it had ever belonged to, and how the toe and its owner were parted.

"It's a copycat crime, Querida," I said. "Just like the finger in the chili at Wendy's."

Same theme, different digit. I am a criminal justice major at California State University, Sacramento. Between my program at Sac State and passion for crime shows, I am onto these things.

Mike, the store manager came, saw, scratched his head and wrung his hands. He ordered his female assistant manager to bring a cloth with ice for Bebe's head while he helped her sit down in a booth several tables away from the scene of the crime. He assured her he had no idea who would do such a sick thing, that TOT met impeccable health and safety standards, and that he would personally do anything it took to make it up to her, including a full refund and a generous gift card to compensate.

"You poor thing, "Mike said to her. "What a shock."

He asked his assistant, Molly, a redhead who was about to graduate from Sac State in social work, to take over calming Bebe while he called the cops.

I came up behind Bebe at the end booth and draped my arms around her neck. I kissed her on the top of her head.

"It'll be OK, Querida. Rest with Molly till the cops come. I'm gonna go look at the thing, just like a CSI."

I know I watch too much television, but at least, thanks to it, I knew I shouldn't contaminate the crime scene. However, I couldn't resist poking the toe with a plastic fork to get a better look at it in all its glory. Fat, brown, probably Hispanic, and hairy. Eeeuwwh! They'd have to run a search in that paint match thingy to see what brand of nail polish it was. I was hoping it'd be odd to narrow the search, as if this weren't odd enough.

Staring at the toe, I flashed on the award Mike proudly displayed on the wall at Tons o' Tacos: voted Best Taqueria this year by *Sacramento News and Review*, a coveted honor.

"Saucy Salsa," I muttered to myself, the name of TOT's nearby rival in Mexican fast food. Could its obnoxious manager have been so envious that he crossed the line, or in this case toed it?

I broke my reverie to look over at Bebe. She and Molly were chatting softly. Suddenly, Bebe burped, covered her mouth and ran for the ladies' room. When she emerged at least ten minutes later, her eyes were all puffy. I could tell she'd been crying as well as barfing.

"What kind of sick could I get from a dead toe?" Bebe asked. "E. coli?"

Thank God, she hadn't actually bitten into it, more like bumped it with her front teeth.

I couldn't resist. "Well, it was the big toe. Toe Main Poisoning?"

Bebe couldn't help but laugh. "You're channeling Tomás."

Tio Tomás, my recently deceased uncle, was a piece of work. A relentless practical joker, Bebe found him less funny than mean, and I'm sure she was irritated at me for imitating his gallows humor, except that I really couldn't. I don't have the edge. Or the evil streak. My poor puns could never hold a candle to Tomás and his meanness. Tomás had faked his death several times for laughs before he finally died for real last month of a coronary. He was in the heat of doing it with some woman he had on the side, not his wife. I was horrified for my auntie. She was a saint who did not deserve that final humiliation.

―――

Later, Bebe complained my enthusiasm for the mystery of her misfortune embarrassed her.

"You were all over the crime scene investigators like an exuberant puppy," she said, "asking too many questions. With your pestering, I can't imagine how they got the toe out of the slop to bag it, much less to concentrate on anything else they were doing."

Bebe was right. The CSIs finally sent me back to the booth where Molly and Bebe were bonding because of the bizarreness of it all. The taqueria was becoming a war zone of dark humor, Tio Tomás style.

Soon after I slid into the booth with the girls, a Captain Holyoke appeared out of nowhere "to ask a few questions." Molly took this as her cue to become scarce and slid out of her side of the booth.

Bebe had already overheard Holyoke, minutes before, grilling the grillers. He had pinned down who had most likely flipped the toe taco. TOT was located within blocks of Sac State and the grill guy in question was a clean-cut, freckle faced kid that looked like Richie Cunningham on Happy Days before he grew up, grew bald and made movies. "Richie" was not smiling. Richie was being lectured by the manager.

Bebe told me she couldn't tell if he had been fired, but she saw the kid walk toward the back of the taqueria, taking off his apron on the way. She felt sorry for him. How could he have known he was dishing up ground beef that wasn't 100 percent USDA Choice?

Captain Holyoke took names, straight out of prime time.

"Jorje Gonzalez," I said.

"Brenda Bradford, but everyone calls me Bebe because of my initials."

Holyoke made notes then sat back against the booth.

"There are two things I have to sort out," he said. "First, was this toe from someone still living when it was severed or are we talking about a dead person? Some of my officers are on that, contacting local funeral parlors and morgues to find out if any bodies are missing a big toe. Second, was the delivery random or aimed at one of you specifically?"

Bebe looked from Holyoke to me, eyes wide. "Who would aim her dead toe at us?"

"Do either of you have enemies?" When Holyoke frowned, deep ruts appeared between his brows. "Someone who'd like to get even with you for something?"

We looked at each other.

"Well, I hate to say it, but Bebe's ex-boyfriend wasn't too happy when we got back together."

"Name?" Holyoke asked Bebe. "And how long did you go with him?"

"Alex Perry," Bebe said without hesitation. "Jorje and I have known each other since we were kids. We needed a break from one another so I started seeing Alex, about eight months ago now. In time, I knew I was still in love with Jorje. We got back together a couple months ago. Six months I saw Alex, tops."

"Any repercussions with this Alex guy?"

"Repercussions?" My voice cracked. "The guy is a freak. He threatened me, he followed and bugged Bebe to the point that we thought we'd have to file a restraining order. Until my Uncle Tomás took care of it."

Captain Holyoke's frown tightened. "Who is this Uncle Tomás, and how did he take care of it?"

So, I told him: "Tomás is my father's brother, Tomás Gonzalez. Tomás died last month."

Captain H. sounded irritated. "How did he take care of it?"

I looked at Bebe and we couldn't suppress our laughter.

"I can't wait to hear what's so funny," Holyoke said, in a tone that dripped sarcasm.

I wiped the laughter off my mouth and went on.

"Tomás worked in a funeral parlor for years. He also had a morbid sense of humor, which he probably got from working there. On top of it, he was an unrelenting practical joker. One night, Tomás broke into Alex's car while he was lurking around at Bebe's, which he was doing almost every night at dark on the dot.

"Tomás left a dummy in the driver's seat looking shot up like the St. Valentine's Day Massacre. Working in the funeral home, he knew how to make fake blood look authentic. He trashed Alex's car in bogus blood, guts and gore. Chicken guts, I suspect. Smashed the windows, too."

"And he left a sticky note on the nose of the dummy referring to me," Bebe volunteered. "It said 'BB Careful.' Alex showed me when he came pounding on my door, screaming."

"I was with Bebe that night," I added. "We wouldn't normally have opened the door, and Alex normally wouldn't have nearly beaten it down, but he sounded so freaked, I went out there to see what happened. He wouldn't let me help him clean it up or drive his car home. I had to call his Mommy to come pick him up."

Holyoke said without taking his eyes off his notes: "And after that?"

"Somebody picked his car up the next day, a friend or relative, I assume. But neither of us have seen or heard from Alex again. I think Tomás scared the crap out of him."

Holyoke scratched more notes. I squeezed Bebe's hand.

"So, this uncle of yours was protective of you and your girlfriend, Jorje?"

"Well, to tell the truth, he was not a warm and fuzzy uncle. His sick humor amused him more than most members of our family, including me. And he did not approve of dating outside our culture, that Bebe isn't Latina. That's why I was surprised when he stepped in like that to help us in his weird way. But Tomás thought Alex was potentially dangerous. "

Holyoke lifted his head: "Then he admitted upfront that he pulled the St. Valentine—"

"Never. But something you have to understand about Tomás. It was signature. There was no missing his work. He did crazy things. No one else could be so creative and macabre at the same time. I don't doubt Alex might have had other enemies, but I'd stake my life on it. This was as good as a canvas signed by the master."

"Okay," the captain said. "You two have been helpful. I'll be in touch."

———

As the days passed, many former fans shunned Tons 'o' Tacos because the toe story was so disgusting. TOT had been a campus hangout so popular with certain students that it had almost become one of them. While some people soon forgot that a live, human co-ed—my precious Bebe!—almost ate that terrible toe and felt that TOT was wronged, the bad press nearly killed the place, a lot of "poor TOT," zero customer loyalty.

Then there was me. No one could keep me away from Tons 'o' Tacos, not even Bebe, who sometimes almost begged on her hands and knees. I know I was making a pest of myself, asking the manager and staff at least every other day if they had heard anything new on the case. I had already worn out my welcome with Captain Holyoke. He no longer returned my calls.

I admit it. I was obsessed. I took to Googling for news items about the case on my laptop several times a day, regardless of where Bebe and I happened to be at the time.

"If this is your idea of what to do in the afterglow," Bebe warned, "you need to get a life. Maybe a new girlfriend."

I could see that the toe story was beginning to strain our relationship, but it was also hot news. Even though the crime was local, it had a relationship to another widespread story, the Wendy's finger, which made every fast food customer feel vulnerable. That made it universal, because who doesn't eat junk food at least now and then? It was ludicrous and darkly comical. Newscasters from coast to coast made horrible jokes. I wanted to put an end to it—to solve the crime—because I felt like the jokes were at Bebe's expense. But Bebe had had enough of it all.

"Jorje," she said, "I don't know what is making me crazier, my national embarrassment, my post-traumatic stress from nearly eating a human toe or you not letting it go for even five minutes. Give it a break. Please?"

That was easier said than done for me, especially when I picked up an important clue from one of my frequent visits to what was left of TOT. Several employees had been fired within weeks before the toe taco incident. One of them was very rough around the edges. He created a big scene when the ax came down. He screamed at Mike, "You'll pay!" The cops were wondering if he axed a toe and planted it for revenge. Any progress toward proving that theory was hush-hush and the suspense was killing me.

I got the name of the disgruntled employee, Andrew Palmer, and started investigating him online and staking out his ramshackle apartment. I was convinced that Palmer was the only reasonable suspect. No one was trying to sue Tons 'o' Tacos like the Wendy's case. This was a vendettoe, a vendetta by an unhinged former taco turner. Plain and simple.

Of course, Bebe didn't have a clue I had gone cloak and dagger. I was quite pleased with myself in my dark glasses and borrowed friend's car, peering around a sunshade on the side window with binoculars. That is, until a rap of metal on metal made me jump three feet out of my seat.

I pulled back the corner of the shade and saw Holyoke.

"Looking for something?" he said.

The captain had his gun unholstered. He had obviously used it to rap me back to reality. Busted and sent home, I was forced to let the cops do their job until I could think of a new way to worm my way into the investigation.

The next day, Bebe and I were driving past TOT on the way to class when we both caught a glimpse of Alex Perry walking in. I skidded to a near stop and peeled in, almost missing the driveway.

"What are you doing?" Bebe yelled.

"You saw him! Alex Perry just ducked in."

"Jorje, don't do this."

"I'm not doin' anything. I'm just watching."

Alex Perry walked out ten minutes later with the Richie Cunningham look-alike. "So they're friends," I said out loud, the light dawning.

I was convinced I had solved the case. Alex Perry had one-upped them with a practical joke sicker than the best of Tio Tomás. I knew who put the toe in the taco and why, a simple case of love spurned and sweet revenge, using his friend who worked at TOT to plant the toe. I doubted Alex could know it was my uncle who pulled the St. Valentine's, but if he had figured it out, he had even more reason to get back at Bebe and me for my uncle's gory warning.

I fished in my wallet for Captain Holyoke's business card.

"Mr. Gonzalez," he said when he answered his phone. "I'm glad you called. I have some updates."

Captain H. went onto say the toe had been frozen, making it difficult to determine when it had been severed from its body, which they were quite sure was dead, by the way. The toenail polish was the cheap 99 cent generic red you could find at any drug store, impossible to trace.

"But here's the interesting part," Holyoke said.

Captain Holyoke's punch line was drowned out by wailing sirens and police car bubble tops making a mad dash entrance into the taqueria parking lot.

"I can't hear you," I protested. "This place is swarming with cop cars."

"I sent them," Holyoke chuckled. "They're there to arrest Ryan Keller, the freckle-faced kid that works there. We think he stuck the toe in the taco."

"Richie Cunningham" finally had a name.

"Alex Perry's friend!"

"Yeah, but that's not why we are arresting him."

"Then why?"

Bebe was waving her arms frantically beside me, mouthing "What, what???" It was driving her crazy that she couldn't hear the cop half of the conversation.

I pitched up the volume on my cell to the max, holding it between our ears. She leaned in close.

"Ryan Keller had two jobs. He was also a gopher at the funeral home and the son of your uncle's lover. They knew each other well."

Our mouths dropped onto the car seat. Bebe's eyes grew rounder than tacos grandes.

I told him, "I am completely confused."

"Come down to the station and I'll tell you the rest."

Bebe and I were delighted to see Alex Perry looking bummed as his friend, Ryan the Freckle Faced Kid, was ducked into the back seat of the cop car and dragged off to jail. I followed the car to the police station, once the knot of cop cars untangled to set us free. Free from Tons 'o' Tacos, its tight fitting little parking lot and its bad memories.

At the police headquarters, Captain Holyoke was enlightening.

"Tomás had heart trouble much worse than he admitted to any members of your family. He knew it was just a matter of time. So, he had a deal with Ryan. After he died, Ryan was to cut off his toe and paint the nail red to stuff it in your taco. He knew you frequented Tons 'o' Tacos, which happened to be Ryan's second job, and it was the perfect practical joke. Ryan delivered the body to the crematorium. He just hacked off the toe, froze it and sent the rest of Uncle Tomás to ashes."

Holyoke chuckled.

"If your uncle were still here, I'm sure he'd pat the kid on the back for a job well done, except for the fact that Bebe took the first taco on the tray, which I think was meant for you."

"But why would Tomás do this to me and Bebe? And how did you find out? You just arrested him."

"Yeah, we just arrested him," Holyoke said. "But when we questioned Alex Perry yesterday, thinking he might be the avenger because of his relationship with Bebe, Alex sang like a lark. Snitched his friend off in a heartbeat. Ryan had confided in him. So there you have it. I'm sure DNA will confirm it. It's your uncle's toe."

"But what about the kid that got fired, Palmer?"

"Never a serious suspect, although we watched him just like you did. Did you find anything?"

Holyoke was making fun of me now, and I knew I deserved it. I had really gotten carried away. I was grateful Holyoke had a sense of humor, considering the man hours wasted on one of my uncle's stupid, morbid practical jokes.

In the end, Tons 'o' Tacos was the victim, just like the regulars complained. Tomás's accomplice, Ryan Keller, was in big trouble. He'd have to pay for damages, lost business, workers laid off and endangering the food supply with my dead uncle's decomposing toe.

Still, I couldn't help but take it personally.

"Why would Tio Tomás do this to me?" I asked Holyoke as if I almost expected him to know.

"You tell me."

Bebe sighed. "We rarely understood his sick humor."

I was clueless at first but offered my only thought.

"Maybe Tomás did not think I acted grateful enough for how he stopped Alex from bothering Bebe. I appreciated his sentiment, but his way of doing it was so inappropriate, not to mention illegal. Imagine busting in and trashing someone's car like that. I hated to encourage him. Tomás made himself hard to love."

Knowing Tomás, he probably gave Ryan some cock-and-bull story about why he wanted to pull this practical joke on his "favorite" nephew. Ryan probably had no clue that Tomás pulled the dummy massacre on his friend Alex or that Tomás was getting even with me for not kissing his feet for the "favor."

One thing was clear. Tomás was craftier than I ever gave him credit for and original, flipping me off from beyond the grave that way, using a different digit than anyone else.

———

A day later, Holyoke called me back into the PD. The fact that he wouldn't tell me about this "new development" over the phone had me really curious.

"Jorje," he said, "I have mixed emotions about telling you the latest, but I'm convinced you'll find out anyway. Ryan Keller is such a blabbermouth, he probably already has a deal with *National Enquirer*. I thought you deserved a heads-up, given your personal involvement in the case and relation to the toe. Thought it might be kinder."

"Captain Holyoke, I cannot imagine what you are talking about."

"His cellmate said Keller had loud nightmares, talking to himself."

What did this have to do with the price of huevos?

"We sat him down for some additional questioning and I guess the horror of what he had experienced came gushing out. Truth is, your uncle was not intact."

I started getting sick to my stomach without even knowing what was coming next.

"Your aunt apparently duped Tomás's key and snuck into the mortuary just as Keller was hacking off her deceased husband's toe. She was waving a knife, cussing up a storm—"

I was getting sicker. My "sweet" Tia Dolores?

"She forced him to hack off something else further up."

The nausea started to seize me.

"I guess she planned to do it herself, but she had heard about Ryan Keller, that Tomás worked with the son of his lover. When she accidentally came upon the kid and saw him already hacking, she went bonkers and seized the opportunity to force him to do the job for her."

"Of course, Ryan cremated Tomás afterwards, so there's no evidence. I'm not sure I'd even bother to arrest either one of them for desecrating human remains, even with his confession."

While the Captain treated me with the utmost respect throughout this information exchange, I could tell at times that he was nearly biting the insides of his mouth to keep from laughing. Who could blame him? I was having the same problem on my seesaw between horror and hilarity. I was dying over how the rest of my family would react when they got wind of it, especially my dad.

I could not ask the next obvious question.

"I suppose you're wondering what happened to, well, it," Holyoke said.

"Your aunt wanted to force him to bring it home to his mother. Keller managed to run and ditch Dolores and later bring all of Tomás's parts to the crematorium except for the toe he'd iced, but the kid has been shaking in his shoes ever since. Your aunt scared the hell out of him."

She had taken so much from that crazy old coot, my uncle, especially his final insult, dying in the bed of another woman. They say couples who have been together many years start looking alike. I have seen it. Whoever thought my aunt and uncle would start acting alike? My angel aunt gone to the devil—

Still, no matter how horrible her deed, there was a part of me so sick of my uncle's pranks, I could not resist giving Tia Dolores a mental thumbs-up.

Reunion

Maggie McMillen

Hadyn, my love,

I know you are wondering why I am writing you a letter. Very little time has ticked by since we promised each other that our slumber party last weekend was not good-bye but hello to our new beginning. I float on cloud nine, maybe ten, waiting for your call, waiting to hear your voice. My cell phone lies on the table next to my hand.

My flight home yesterday was routine except that I soared higher than the plane. I felt you filling the seat beside me, leaning close to share a thought, your breath on my cheek. I felt your hand squeeze mine to make me feel safe as we lifted off. I saw your brown eyes twinkle at me, heard your laugh invite me to join you in a foolish joke. I felt your shoulder brush mine when the plane hit turbulent air. The captain's reassuring voice on the intercom was yours.

I smelled your aftershave and trembled at the essence of you, sheltered in my soul. I re-lived our first kiss after twenty years apart and the hair on my arms stood up. My skin, my body, my heart responded to the memory of your touch. You are more than a portrait in my mind. You are a part of me.

I've heard it said that you can't go home again, but you and I, Hadyn, proved that old saw doesn't sing. It's as though we never parted, as if that day so long ago didn't happen. That day, you blindsided me with your words, "I think we should see others."

"Mrs. Maynard?"

"Jannica, please. Everyone calls me Jannica."

"More coffee? Water?"

———

"Thanks, no, I'm fine. Shall I leave? Do you need this table?" I smiled.

"No."

"I'll just finish my letter and go along then. I have things to do at home."

———

Hadyn, I missed you. I missed us. Only you ever breathed, "Nicci, Nicci," your special name for me, on the back of my neck and pressed kisses into my hair. Can you believe it's been two decades? Twenty years of painful moments brushed away in a kiss that felt like we were apart for only an eye blink. After Rafe's wake last Saturday, we picked up our romance without awkward gaps and meaningless words. My shock and hurt at your sudden whim to leave me were set aside in that first new kiss.

Though we both moved on after you left me, I have the strangest idea that our reunion was our first time together. How odd is that? Maybe it was just more meaningful this time around.

I'm happy inside, hugging myself, as I dust off my memories of us. I should feel sad about the circumstances that brought the three of us, Rafe, you and me, together again, but you crowd my feelings about Rafe's death out of my head.

Rafe, faithful, loyal friend, Rafe. His funeral in our old home town, especially the interment, seems surreal and shadowy. Is it just one of those nitwitted tricks we pulled growing up? Or real, like Laurie's funeral. Remember? Her casket was closed because she catapulted out of Rafe's convertible into a rotting log as we raced along Ocean Beach during Easter break. No amount of tulle could hide her injuries, we were told. We grieved by cramming into a booth at the Talking Parrot, drinking tall cherry cokes and smoking our brains out.

We three were something, weren't we? The Triad, we called ourselves back then, cruising neighborhood streets in Rafe's jalopy or yours, whichever one was in running order at the time, looking for fun. We spent hours after school at the Parrot, gossiping and lamenting over strict parents. Or we jammed into the streetcar full of swaying bodies to ride across the river to hang out downtown and annoy shopkeepers.

I know, Hadyn, Rafe was your friend first since third grade, but I leaned on his strong shoulder when you left me for all those "others" you planned to date. I hoped you'd sow your oats and come back. I broke into fragments when you married. I guess I can write Penny. You married Penny. There it is written. And you have two sons. I moved away and married and I have a daughter. Our lives continued, just not the way we planned and I hoped.

Coincidence can't explain where we find ourselves now. Things happen when they are supposed to. Our time wasn't then, but it is now, my dear, sweet friend and lover.

Last weekend was exciting, daring even. We opened the door to a fresh start for us, the sequel us, Hadyn.

Nostalgia for the past overwhelms me as I knit this afghan of stale memories. Bits and pieces of our shared past pop in and out of my head, a bouncing ball of faded yarn unwinding to reveal a bygone time. But we each bring bright skeins to weave into our new pattern.

I'm reminded of the argyle sock fad back in our dating years. Girls knitted argyle footwear for boys, colorful socks like harlequins that peeped out between polished brogans and yellow cords to verify who was going steady.

In my mind's eye I saw a perfectly patterned pair of socks, a symbol of my undying love. In my hands I held a snarl of multi-colored yarns dangling on bobbins from knitting needles, a jumbled mass. The project, kindled by teen-age hot pants, failed. I confess I never got past the first sock. You and a mythical second sock vied for my attention till I lost interest in knitting socks. Instead, you pinned my sweater with a sweetheart fraternity pin to prove we were a couple.

Growing up, we shared friends, teachers, streets, schools, parks, games, laughter, and love in our own miniature universe. We rode our bikes to the same hangouts, swam in the same public pool at Freestone Park, necked at the same Friday night make-out parties at JoHana's house. Now we can laugh about the look of surprise on Jo's mother's face when she left work early and came home to a dark house. She snapped on the light and found twenty kids sprawled on her living room floor, necking and feeling each other up. Apoplexy doesn't do her reaction justice. Mama grounded me for a month.

We sat on the same hard grandstand benches to cheer our high school football team to victory in the rain. You drove us fifty miles to the state capitol for the basketball playoffs and championship games. Rafe and a dozen kids crowded into the back of your dad's moving van like illegal aliens. I sat beside you on the bench seat littered with Lucky Strike packs, book matches, Hershey candy bar wrappers, and a dirty, torn road map. My hand covered yours on the red gearshift knob. At the games, leaning side by side against the rail of the overhead indoor track, you taught me to French kiss.

Remember the winter our two families shared a skiing vacation at the Lodge on Mt. Hood in Oregon? We skied and you caught me to shove snow under my jacket, next to my bare skin. Your hands were icy thrills against my warm body. You pelted me with snow balls. Laughing and yelling, chasing and grabbing, we scrambled into the Lodge to snuggle on comfy couches and drank hot cocoa in front of the stone fireplace, big enough to walk into. I sneaked looks at you to see if you knew you touched my breast.

Daddy sucked up the last drops of bourbon he packed in his suitcase and took up space on a bar stool guzzling beer, not even pretending to hit the slopes. With the secret out of the box that my father drank, I was embarrassed and devastated. I worried you'd hear gossip about the accident with the train, discover the arrests, learn my mother drove him because his license was suspended, or find out how my uncle really got the scar on his cheek.

I still hear the clank of cables in that creaky elevator stinking of derelict urine when we were seventeen. The grungy hotel was cheaper than Nob Hill by a ton, you said. After you pushed the dirty console button that forced the elevator cage to lunge up or jolt down, you wiped your pointy finger on my blouse to rub germs on me as a tease. You unlocked the door to a dark, damp and dingy room. I was upset and scared. You held me and stopped my tears with kisses and made everything sunny and funny. We were together, young and in love, the first day of forever.

We welcomed college, the best years of our lives, a time to fly from our nests. Our parents sent us off with visions of stuffing the world in our pockets. But the world slipped from my fingers.

As I write, I can smell San Francisco. It was your idea to live in The City, where we grew up, all on our own after graduation. Neither set of parents were pleased, urging marriage as a better alternative. But we were rebels back then.

The pungent sting of fog rolling in and wetting the streets still lingers up my nose. I feel the steamy warmth of the quaint café we claimed as "our place," with meaty barbecue exhaust puffing out of sidewalk vents. I was romantic. I said I could smell sunshine on the wharf and Bay but you said it was just hot tar in the street.

Your car was unreliable, grunting up the steep hills or careening down toward the Bay. We were never sure if the brakes would hold. We felt safer riding cable cars in pale lemon sun and gray foggy mists. Cable bells clanged in our ears. On chilly nights breezes chapped our lips and pinked our cheeks. Across the Bay, we counted magic pinpoints of light like fireflies flickering against the skyline, I said. Earthbound stars, you said.

When Islamic fanatics in Tehran took American hostages, Mama's youngest brother in the Army was shipped to the Middle East where military action threatened. You talked about enlisting. I didn't want you to go and we argued.

I hate disputes. I heard too many drunken challenges at home between my parents. Mama swore she drank to keep Daddy from being too boozy to do more than sit in his chair and stare at nothing. Mama's cheeks burned red after slamming down straight whiskey, a dead giveaway to her degree of inebriation along with her voice that grew harsh and a laugh that cut the room in two. She threw back her head and tossed down jiggers as neat as Daddy. Mama's copycat tippling only lacked Daddy's gruff throat clearing, "Ahhhh," as the liquor burned his gullet.

My family never drove anywhere without a pint of whiskey or maybe two in the glove compartment, Daddy's liquor locker. He'd need a little drinkie every ten miles or so and Mama drank with him, shot for shot. To save him from getting snockered, she said.

You promised to rescue me, Hadyn, and you did till—what? What happened? Wanderlust or pure lust? I never saw it coming. If you left clues, I missed them. I was so lost in love I would have missed a house falling on me. When it did fall, I was crushed.

Our sweet reunion after Rafe was put to rest seems more poignant now and sticks in my mind like an ear worm, a snatch of song that won't go away.

I hope to know the people in your life, Hadyn. I'd like you to know my daughter who is studying in Paris. Something to arrange when we get together again?

Capital Crimes

I see my life as pages of tiny ornate script, meticulously documented by an ancient, wizened monk in a musty monastery. The scribe's back hurts, his fingers are cramped and arthritic. The rough paper tears hangnails and slices tiny, smarting cuts on his soft fingers. His eyes are dim and watery from tedious entries in my life book in a windowless cell by candlelight. The monk spends uncounted hours diligently compiling my life path. The volume is stiff, the spine unbroken. No one but the Argus-eyed monk, alert to every aspect, nicety and nuance, has turned the pages. The book carries the smell of old leather and the monk stacks it atop other life works on God's desk beside His elbow. God nudges the stack. Manuscript pages slip to the floor. God picks up the papyrus sheets and idly inserts the leaves between the covers of my book out of order. God is too busy to sort pages into proper sequence or to make sure they are mine. Often I do things too late or ahead of time in random order and repeat lessons already learned, but I know it's up to me to make order of the chaotic jumble.

Dearest Hadyn, I have much to do at home.

———

I capped the pen, laid it on the yellow legal tablet and rubbed my eyes to push away the sleepy feeling that suddenly overpowered me. The door to the interrogation room swung open and the second detective returned with coffee for her partner and herself.

"Ah, Mrs. Maynard, Jannica, you've finished?"

I looked up and smiled. "Almost." I picked up the pen, examined it. "Nice pen. It's like one my husband, Rafe, favored. Flows smoothly and has a good feel in my hand, sturdy and

128

comfortable. Rafe said a good pen puts thoughts in good order. He was a wise man."

I scratched a few more words and handed the pad and pen to the detective sitting across the table from me. I picked up my cell phone and stood up to go.

The detective smiled, held my letter to Hadyn and read my last scribbles: *I knew you'd never call me, my dear Hadyn. I am not sorry I shot you last Saturday and left you to die alone in that lovely hotel room, a lofty step above our first room together. I regret I didn't pull the trigger twenty years ago when you replaced me with those "others." I treasure the surprise on your face when you learned the truth about Hadly, our daughter.*

See you in hell, my love,
Nicci

Tea Time

Cindy Sample

"I recommend arsenic," said Lila Gordon. "It's the easiest way to murder your husband."

"I prefer something slower," said the white haired cherubic-faced grandmother across the table from me. "Like nicotine poisoning."

She flicked her bright gray eyes at me. "What's your favorite poison, dear?"

"Umm— My favorite is—" The brittle raisin scone I had inhaled two seconds earlier lodged in my throat. My hands flailed as I searched for a waitress to refill my water glass.

Twenty-nine members of the Sacramento Mystery Book Club turned to stare at the person rude enough to disturb the discussion of their latest book, a mystery entitled *Digitalis in the Darjeeling*.

When I had managed to clear my throat, I addressed the group.

"Sorry. I haven't read the latest *Poison for Dummies Guide*, I said with a chuckle, hoping a little levity would lighten the tension at the table. "I'd better be careful what I eat and drink with this group."

My mother nudged me. "Jessie, are you trying to alienate my supporters?" Election of the club's officers would be held at this meeting and my mother was determined to unseat Lila Gordon, the current president.

My sister, Denise, jumped in to give me her typical support. "Jessie, you have no idea what a prominent position president of the Sacramento Mystery Book Club is. I'm hoping to become an officer myself someday. Greg thinks it will enhance our social standing."

Since the social standing of my thirty-five year old sister and her dull stuffy husband, Gregory Bainbridge III, MD, was probably zero, any activity would definitely enhance it.

"And it's about time Lila Gordon stopped running every important club in this city," complained Denise.

"Sshsh," my mother reprimanded my sister. "That woman has bionic hearing."

I turned to look at the woman gracing the head of our table. Her expensive cornflower blue hat, covered with silk flowers in a paler shade of blue which perfectly matched her shoes and purse, had obviously not been purchased at Kmart. My one and only beige straw hat, which was perched on my sun streaked dirty blonde hair, had been picked up at a local flea market, the source of most of my post-divorce wardrobe these days.

When the waitress appeared with a teapot, Lila watched to make sure no errant drop of tea landed on her beautiful blue wool suit.

"There's no sweetener, young lady," Lila said in a harsh voice.

"Yes, ma'am. I'll see if we have more." The petite young multi-pierced waitress dropped the teapot on the table with a clatter and scurried into the back of the building.

Lila frowned. "I'm going to have to talk to the owner about her poor service."

My mother stood and walked over to an unoccupied table. She picked up the container of white sugar packets and blue sweeteners and placed it in front of Lila.

"For you, Lila," she said. "You can use a little sweetener."

Lila gave her a dirty look and grudgingly reached for the small white tray. She poured the contents of two pale blue packets into her tea, sipped from the rose patterned teacup and smiled. "I order their Amaretto tea every time I come here. I just love that almond taste."

I took a gulp of my plain old Earl Grey. Boring. Next time I came I'd try the Amaretto myself.

Our server began delivering the three-tiered trays that held the pint-sized finger foods for which the tearoom was well known. She plunked the tray right under Lila's nose. Lila was too engrossed reaching for the sandwiches in front of her to notice the hostile look on the young server's face.

I gazed at the three tiny sandwiches comprising my teatime lunch. The first sandwich was easily recognizable egg salad. One of the other two was covered with green goop, the third one slathered with a black paste. Yuck. I tentatively bit into the unappealing green sandwich. Surprisingly tasty. The black triangular shaped treat was next, a yummy olive tapenade.

I took a quick peek around the table to see if anyone would notice if I snuck some of their sandwiches onto my plate. I glanced at Lila out of the corner of my eye. Definitely didn't want her to see me sneaking treats.

Her plate was empty and she was staring at it with a bemused expression on her face. It was amazing how her blue hat combined with the blue suit tinted her face blue.

Her mouth opened and she emitted an unearthly bellow. Twenty-nine pairs of eyes turned to the woman seated at the head of the table. Her arms thrashed and her head jerked back with such force that her chair flipped backward, flinging her on the floor.

I jumped out of my chair but halted when Susan Starkey brushed past me.

"Step back and give her air, please." Susan, a nurse for many years, knelt down beside the figure that was no longer thrashing about but lying much too still on the floor.

"Call 911," she shouted.

Various pre-set melodies rang out as the women turned on their cell phones and started punching in the emergency number.

Susan checked Lila's pulse in her carotid artery and her wrist, the wrist that was now the identical shade of blue as the hat that had flown to the floor like a gigantic blue Frisbee. She shook her head and solemnly addressed our small group.

"Lila's dead," she announced.

A plate of dishes crashed to the ground and our server ran out of the tearoom. I gazed longingly at the lost chocolate opportunity littering the floor then turned my attention back to the group. As the women of the book club looked nervously at each other, I did what I normally do in awkward situations: I inserted my size ten foot into my mouth.

Looking down at my empty plate, I said, "Do you think it was food poisoning?"

Dishes scraped as the women who ate more slowly than I had pushed their plates away. The members began whispering among themselves. Minnie Mason, the cherubic white haired woman seated across from me, started twirling the inch long white hair dangling from her chin.

My sister, ever tactful, blurted out, "I guess this means Mom is the new president."

My mother's cheeks flushed as she frowned at my sibling. "Denise, this is such a tragedy. Minnie, didn't Lila have a bad heart?"

Minnie's fingers stopped twiddling as her sharp gray eyes fastened on my mother and sister. "I know she saw a cardiologist for some chest pain not that long ago. I think he prescribed something."

The slender wrinkle-free woman who had been seated next to Lila attempted to lift her eyebrows at Minnie. Her doctor was evidently very skilled in giving Botox injections because not a muscle moved on her smooth forehead.

"Lila's husband will be devastated," she said, looking appropriately devastated herself as she twisted the snow globe-sized diamond ring on her right hand.

Minnie snorted. "Are you kidding? He'll probably be dancing all the way to the mortuary. Lila had all the money in their family and she was a first-class bitch to him." Minnie snapped her fingers. "If Lila said jump, Russ jumped."

I jumped myself as the Dutch door to the tea shoppe crashed open. Two EMT's followed by two police officers, a man and a woman, shouldered their way into the room. The paramedics started examining Lila.

"I'm Detective Mueller," said the tall, broad shouldered, sandy haired male officer. "Who's in charge?"

We looked around the table. Several of the women pointed to Lila's prone form.

"That's our president," said Minnie, pointing to the blue-on-blue corpse.

He rolled his eyes and sighed.

"Who's next in command?" he asked in a grating voice.

The black-suited botoxed beauty waved at the detective. "I'm the club secretary and I've been a member for over twenty years. Would you like to interview me?" she asked, not missing an opportunity to flash a seductive smile.

My sister, the princess of suck up, popped out of her chair. "My mother is the vice president. Obviously she should assume the responsibilities of president."

My mother attempted to look modest but I could see she was excited about the attention from the detective. She slid her chair back, stood and gazed around the table at the other club members.

"Ladies, shall we take a vote?" she asked the group.

Detective Mueller placed a beefy hand on Mom's shoulder. "Lady, how about we deal with the dead woman first. Then you can have your vote." He looked disgusted with our whole group.

I was feeling disgusted with the politicking myself. These ladies needed to get their priorities in order.

The police officers must have agreed with my assessment. Detective Mueller and his female counterpart, Detective Brady, separated the club members from each other and asked each of us to give a statement. The paramedics moved Lila into the ambulance for her final ride to that great tearoom in the sky.

The interviews were relatively brief. No one had seen anything or knew anything. It turned out that despite her longevity at the helm of the Book Club, most of the women had been loyal to Lila more out of fear than friendship. Evidently Lila had a nasty habit of collecting dirt on her "friends" and she wasn't above using the information to maintain her place in society.

Despite the fact that I barely knew Lila, I found it difficult to make eye contact with Detective Mueller while he questioned me. My libido, which had been in hibernation for over a year, had activated at a most unconventional time. I hoped my blushing cheeks didn't move me to the top of the suspect list.

The detective was courteous but all business. After a brief interview, it appeared that I was neither a suspect, nor a prospect. Too bad. I wouldn't have minded meeting the detective again, under different circumstances.

——

Ten days later, I found myself once again surrounded by the members of the Sacramento Mystery Book Club. Instead of a tearoom, we were seated in hard backed pews, compliments of the Heavenly Haven Mortuary.

Lila's husband had gone all out for his wife, either out of love and respect, or relief at her demise. Her closed casket was a shiny steel blue, and large urns of blue and lilac hued flowers lined the sides of the large chapel.

Lila's cardiologist had confirmed that she suffered from congestive heart failure. The coroner had completed the autopsy, which showed an excess of nitroglycerin in her system. Since the medicine had recently been prescribed for her condition, the police department closed the case and called it an accidental overdose.

As her minister summarized Lila's worthy accomplishments, I glanced around the room. I would like to say there wasn't a dry eye in the house, but I couldn't find any wet ones. No soggy hankies crumpled up in any of the mourner's hands. Most of the faces bore similar expressions: relief or boredom.

I slid closer to Denise and tried to get a better look at the widower. Denise frowned at me and I almost stuck my tongue out at her. Old habits are hard to break. We were seated only seven rows behind Russ Gordon. He was sitting next to a black-haired woman. A family member? He whispered in the woman's ear and she turned and smiled at him. My mouth opened in surprise. It was the botoxed beauty who had sat next to Lila in the tearoom the afternoon of her death.

Today the woman was clad in another beautiful black suit. Was that suspicious? Owning two black designer suits? My mother was wearing the same navy suit and hat she had worn to the tearoom the day Lila died. I had borrowed a dark burgundy dress from Denise, fearing that my multi-colored handkerchief-edged skirts and bright pastel sweaters were probably not the most appropriate wear for this somber occasion.

I eyed Russ and his companion, neither of whom looked remotely sad. Could they have conspired to poison Lila? Could she have slipped some of the medication from Lila's purse into her teacup?

Since the police were no longer investigating a homicide, I wondered if the detective would attend the service. I swiveled to the left then the right, locked eyes with Detective Mueller and blushed. Again.

Guilty, but only of lust.

The service was over in less than forty minutes. Other than her husband and her minister, no one else took the opportunity to extol Lila's virtues, or lack thereof. After the service, we gravitated to another room for light refreshments. I stood in a corner watching the different cliques of women. Everyone looked much too happy. My mother and Denise were in their element mingling with the other Mystery Book Club members.

I didn't see any sign of the widower or the black suited botoxed beauty. Should I point out their absence to Detective Mueller?

Speaking of the Detective, he had slipped in right next to me with a plate of hors d'oeuvres and a plastic cup of punch in hand.

"Jessie, you look very introspective," he said as he popped a mini quiche in his mouth.

"Oh, Detective Mueller," I said. "I've been noticing the absence of grief in this room. I barely knew Lila but it's really sad. Are you still investigating? Or am I allowed to ask?"

He shook his head. "The coroner ruled it an accident. Do I agree with him? I'm not at liberty to say. But there were a lot of people with motive and opportunity. Lila Gordon was a very unpopular woman."

He licked some of the flaky pastry from his fingers. Nice capable hands, I thought, not that it was any of my business.

His hazel eyes met mine. "Jessie, now that you're not a suspect, would you like to get together for coffee some time?"

My mouth opened, shut, opened, and finally went into operational mode.

"Um, sure, I'd like that. Call me."

"I will. I have your number." He smiled and went back to canvassing the room.

What were the odds of meeting a man I was attracted to during a murder investigation? It was just like one of those romantic mysteries I liked to read late at night, the ones where the amateur sleuth solves the case and impresses the handsome police detective.

I floated over to my mother and her entourage. Denise had already left. The little woman had to get dinner ready for her pompous husband. I was listening to one of the many "Lila Gordon" stories when I remembered that I had forgotten to tell Detective Mueller of my suspicions about Russ Gordon and the gorgeous beauty in the black suit.

Through the window, I could see that dark clouds had filled the sky. I moved closer to the window and pulled aside the heavy maroon velour drapes to see if the storm coming our way had begun to pelt the pavement yet.

And there they were, the widower and the botoxed beauty, by the silver Mercedes. He was helping her into the car. They were getting ready to drive off together. I looked for Detective Mueller but he must have already departed. Someone had to follow them.

My mother wasn't eager to be dragged away from her entourage, so I yanked her arm and told her I'd left the window open in her new BMW. The skies were now filled with churning charcoal clouds. Dead leaves formed miniature funnels that swirled around the asphalt.

We rushed out of the chapel but were too late. My shoulders slumped as the Mercedes roared out of the parking lot and turned down the highway. Had Lila's murderers escaped?

I walked over to a cement bench and plunked down in defeat. My mother was scurrying over to her car. Nothing like a potential drenching to make that woman hustle. I chuckled when a huge gust of wind blew off her navy hat. The broad brimmed hat, trimmed with a wide navy satin band, bounced along the pavement.

Bounce, bounce, bounce.

With each bounce, a tiny blue packet was ejected from the satin band. I stared at the packets in disbelief. The tiny pale blue squares formed a trail that led right up to…my mother.

The murderer?

Doggie Style Dead

Linda Joy Singleton

I hit the brakes, rolled to a stop and yelled, "Get in the car!"

Jeff, my co-worker at Grants Vet Clinic in Midtown Sacramento, looked at me like I was crazy. And maybe I was, but if I hadn't done something, Tiffany would be dead.

"What's this about?" Jeff asked, slipping on his seatbelt as I drove away from his house. "Do you know how late it is? I was about ready to get in the shower when you called."

I felt my cheeks redden as the image of six-foot, blue-eyed, muscular Jeff in a shower did a movie close-up in my head. Stop it, Micqui! I told myself firmly. Sure Jeff is hot, but he's just a friend and Amber said he already has a girlfriend.

"What are you doing with that?" Jeff pointed to a syringe sticking out of my pocket. I'd "borrowed" a sedative, about four doses more than I'd need, from work just in case I had any trouble with Tiffany. I'd already broken so many rules, one more hardly mattered.

A sharp sound came from the back of my car. Jeff took one look into the backseat and nearly freaked. "Tiffany! What is she doing here? She's supposed to be dead!"

At the sound of her name, cute blonde Tiffany lunged forward and landed on Jeff's lap. She yapped and starting licking Jeff's face, getting closer to Jeff than I ever would. Right then I knew I really must be nuts, not because I'd broken rules and rescued Tiffany from being gassed, but because I was totally envying the poodle for sitting on Jeff's lap.

"Out with it, Micqui," Jeff said, patting Tiffany's curly head. "You were instructed to put Tiffany down this afternoon. Dr. Herald could be sued if Tiffany's owner finds out you didn't do it. You've risked everyone at Grants Veterinary Clinic over one dog."

"But I couldn't let her die!" I turned a corner and accelerated. "It's wrong to kill a healthy young dog just because her owner says she's vicious. This is not a vicious dog."

Tiffany jumped up and licked Jeff's mouth. "That's for sure," he laughed. "For a dog, Tiffany is a total pussy cat."

"That's not the only reason I took her," I admitted. "I don't think Mrs. Strassmore ordered her death. A neighbor brought Tiffany in and showed a signed paper from Mrs. Strassmore, authorizing us to put the dog down. The neighbor said Tiffany had turned vicious and Mrs. Strassmore was too overcome with grief at her husband's death to come herself. But I don't believe it. Add up the fact that Tiffany was growling at the neighbor and Mrs. Strassmore is a rich widow, and it equals attempted doggie-murder. And the neighbor, Mr. Butler, did it!"

"You've been reading too many mystery novels," Jeff said. "What do you plan to do now? Other than get us both fired."

I slowed for a red light and wondered if I'd been wrong to involve Jeff. Sure, I'd needed help and he was the only one I knew who loved animals more than people, just like I did. But it wasn't fair to drag him into my problem. "Sorry. I didn't mean to risk your job. If you want to go back home, I'll take you."

"And miss out on all the fun?" He flashed a grin. "No way! I can always get another job. You've got yourself an accomplice."

With a sigh of relief and a flutter in my heart, I told him my plan. By the time I'd finished, we'd reached our destination: Mrs. Strassmore's estate. Now we just had to figure out how to get over the towering spiked-rail fence.

Jeff tried to climb up one of the slippery rails, but he couldn't get a grip and when I tried to stop his fall, he tumbled on top of me. I didn't complain, just made sure the syringe in my pocket was undamaged and tried to pretend I didn't enjoy our brief physical contact. It was hard to stop smiling.

"The gate is locked," Jeff pointed out.

"There must be some way in. We have to find out if Mrs. Strassmore is okay. I think Mr. Butler forged her signature and is plotting something sinister. I already tried to call Mrs. Strassmore, but there was no answer."

Jeff nodded grimly. "I hope we're not too late."

"At least Tiffany is safe," I said. At the sound of her name, Tiffany yapped and tugged at my pants. "Stop it, Tiff. I can't play now." But the dog chomped down on the edge of my jeans and pulled.

"She wants you to follow her," Jeff said. "I bet she knows a way in."

I figured Tiffany was being a flirt and showing off for Jeff, but sure enough, Tiffany had found an opening. A section of fence bordering Mr. Butler's run-down property was broken. Tiffany zoomed into the hole and vanished.

It took longer for Jeff and me to crawl through, since we had to get down on our knees and duck under thick bushes. When we stood up on the other side, I caught a glimpse of white fur streaking away. Only Tiffany wasn't headed for her owner's home, she dove under another fence right into Mr. Butler's property. I hadn't saved Tiffany's butt only to let her rush back into the waiting arms of her executioner. If Mr. Butler found her, we were all dead meat.

Jeff and I took off in pursuit. "She's going to that garden!" Jeff said as he helped me climb over a rickety fence.

"Looks more like a graveyard." I shivered at the creepy thorn bushes and decaying clumps of dead leaves. A willow tree hunched over the fence in defeat; its limp branches dangling onto Mrs. Strassmore's property. Tiffany had stopped at the willow's trunk and was digging.

"Maybe it is a graveyard," Jeff said ominously, bending down next to Tiffany and pointing to the damp dirt. "This area has been dug up recently. How exactly did Mrs. Strassmore's husband die?"

"A heart attack. And he was buried last week."

"So if this is a grave, it's not the rich husband."

"But maybe it's his wife!" I cried, staring in horror as Tiffany pawed up piles of dirt. "No wonder Mr. Butler wanted to get Tiffany out of the way. The dog clearly hated him. I couldn't believe Mrs. Strassmore would ever hurt her precious Tiffany. She and her husband treated Tiffany like their own child, dressing her up in cute outfits and taking her everywhere. It's Mr. Butler who wanted Tiffany put to sleep."

"Only you couldn't do it." Jeff gently touched my hand. "You broke rules and risked your job to save a dog. I really admire that."

"You do?" My hand tingled from his touch and my heart raced.

"Yeah." He paused. "Maybe when this is over, we could go out sometime."

"But what about your girlfriend?"

He gave me a puzzled look. "What girlfriend?"

"The one Amber told me you had."

"Amber was wrong."

Or lying, I thought, guessing that Amber was angry when Jeff wasn't interested in her, so she made up a story about a girlfriend to save her reputation and keep Jeff away from me. It would have worked except for Tiffany.

"Tiffany's found something!" Jeff exclaimed, pulling a white stick from the ground. But it wasn't a stick.

"A bone! What if it's human?" I choked out just as there was a shout and a deafening blast of a rifle.

Jeff and I jumped up to see Mr. Butler storming out of his house, holding a rifle and shouting at us.

"He's trying to kill us!" I shouted. "Like he probably killed Mrs. Strassmore!"

"Hurry, climb the tree!" Jeff ordered, scooping Tiffany in his arms and swinging up the willow tree.

I grabbed a branch and scrambled up the tree. I hadn't climbed a tree since I was nine, and I bumped my head on a branch and nearly fell out. But another blast from Mr. Butler's rifle made me climb faster. Once on the other side of the fence, I tumbled to the ground.

Jeff let go of Tiffany and reached for my hand. "You okay?"

"For now." I brushed off my aching backside. "We've got to get out of here."

"Yeah. There must be a housekeeper or someone at the Strassmore house who will help."

I nodded, totally out of breath. I heard a shout and caught a glimpse of Mr. Butler's furious face. I didn't waste another second and ran with Jeff.

Tiffany led us up the steps of the Victorian house then disappeared through a square doggie-door. Jeff reached the human door first and started pounding. I pounded, too, our voices mingling with cries of, "Help!"

It seemed like we waited forever, but it was only seconds before an elderly woman wearing a gold robe over a silk nightgown opened the door.

"Mrs. Strassmore!" I cried joyfully. "You're alive!"

"That's not all I am," she replied in a sharp, suspicious tone. "What's the meaning of this? You look familiar. Do I know you?"

Tiffany yapped and jumped up on a couch. I pointed to the poodle and said proudly, "I work at Grants Veterinary Clinic and I rescued your dog. Mr. Butler tried to have her put to sleep."

"That's absurd! He's a very dear friend of mine. He spent hours trying to help me find my Tiffany."

"It was all an act," I told her. "I bet he wants to marry you for your money and he might have even murdered your husband. Tiffany dug up a bone in his garden, so there could be a mass grave with lots of victims."

"Murder? Graves? My goodness, this is a shock." Mrs. Strassmore put her hand to her mouth. "I can't believe Oscar, Mr. Butler, is violent. But he lied to me about Tiffany, so that much is true. He said she'd run away. You better come inside."

"He was shooting at us," Jeff said, looking out in the yard as he shut the door. "I'll call the police."

"Wait here while I get the phone." She disappeared into the kitchen and returned a moment later with a small black object in her hands. Only it wasn't a phone.

"Tiffany was actually my husband's dog," she said. "I'm more of a cat person." The elderly woman aimed the ugly black gun at us. "The police will feel sorry for a poor frightened widow. It's unfortunate that you broke into my house and I mistook you for burglars and accidentally shot you."

"What?" I blinked, sure this couldn't be happening.

"Put your hands behind your backs and don't move." She spoke with deadly calm. "Mr. Butler may be a poor shot, but I never miss my target. My daddy didn't leave me money like my dearly departed husband, but he made sure I could shoot straight before I could ride a bike."

"You killed your husband," Jeff accused.

"Someone had to." She shrugged as if shaking off a fly. "He was such a bore and he treated that bitch Tiffany better than me. I had to beg for even the smallest diamond brooch or trip to Europe. All I had to do was adjust his medication and

149

now I'm free to spend as I please. I already have a flight booked to Paris."

I'd rather she talk than shoot, so I blurted out, "Is Mr. Butler going, too?"

"That lout! Most definitely not." She scowled. "I conned him into believing Tiffany was vicious so he'd get rid of her for me. But he couldn't even do that right. I should have just shot her myself, but I didn't want to look suspicious. Once again, Tiffany is screwing up my life."

Her gaze shifted to the dog who had curled up peacefully on a velvet pillow. Before I realized what was happening, Jeff had taken this chance to dive towards Mrs. Strassmore. She dodged quickly and Jeff went sprawling to the floor, crashing into a lamp. Glass flew everywhere, and as Mrs. Strassmore shielded her face, the gun dropped.

She bent down and picked up the gun, turning ominously toward Jeff. Her back faced me and my brain screamed in panic. Do something! But how could I fight someone with a gun? If I tackled her the gun might go off and hit Jeff. If I didn't, the gun was sure to go off and hit Jeff.

If only I had a weapon— But maybe I did.

I reached into my pocket and fumbled for the syringe. Before I could think clearly, I aimed the syringe and rushed forward. Mrs. Strassmore screamed when the needle stabbed her butt. She jerked back and Jeff kicked the gun out of her hand. She swore and clutched her butt, squirming in anger and pain. Jeff grabbed the gun and aimed it on her, but she'd already crumpled to the ground.

"Wow!" he called out to me. "What did you hit her with?"

I waved the syringe in the air like a victory flag. "She got what she deserved," I told him. "I put her to sleep."

———

A week later, Tiffany had another bone. It was a large rawhide one I'd purchased from the pet shop. Nothing but the best for my little Tiffany. With one of her owner's dead and the other in jail, Tiffany was all mine.

It turned out Tiffany liked to bury her bones, especially in gardens. Mr. Butler apologized for shooting at us. He explained he was only trying to scare us off, that he thought we were vandalizing his property. He seemed relieved to find out Tiffany would be living miles away from his garden.

On the bad side, I lost my job. Dr. Herald was more mad about my "borrowing" the syringe than rescuing Tiffany. Fortunately, Jeff didn't lose his. And I found a new one working for an animal rescue society. It seems I have a talent in that direction.

To celebrate my new career, I went out on my first official date with Jeff. We had a picnic at a beautiful lake with a nice sandy beach perfect for digging.

Jeff, Tiffany and I had a wonderful time.

In Search of Millie

Nancy Streukens

Millie was a trial, always had been and probably always would be until the day she died. I scanned the parking lot for what seemed like the hundredth time, then in desperation counted the old people in the van again. Yep, one still missing. Damn!

Shenandoah Cellars just off Highway 49 loomed at the edge of the parking lot. It was almost noon and the day was turning into a scorcher in the Sierra foothills. Perhaps not the suffocating heat that you'd expect in the humid Midwest or Deep South, but hot enough to sear your feet through your sandals and suck all coherent thought from your brain except the throbbing desire for a frosty can of diet soda. I fanned my face with a wrinkled tour brochure and blew an angry huff of air up towards my forehead. Then I swept my long hair back off my neck and crammed it into a pony tail scrunchie. It made me feel a little cooler but not the least bit better.

It was obvious that Millie was missing and probably wouldn't be showing up anytime soon. I had to go find her. We were finished with our wine tasting tour, two wineries in three hours. We were hot, we were tired. It was time to go home.

I'm positive that search and rescue wasn't included in my job description when I got hired as a summer temporary care companion at the Sunshine Senior Center. But somehow I figured it was something they expected me to do anyway. I mean if you take nine old people out for a field trip, you probably

153

should bring nine old people back in relatively the same condition. Sounded easy on the face of things, but it wasn't. Someone was always getting lost; usually it was Millie.

I looked into the van again. The engine was idling so that the air conditioning could run. Eight old relics from the geriatric generation sat immobile for the most part, slack-jawed, eyes vacant, a testament to the endurance of the old. Mr. Latrowski's hand rested protectively on a bottle of wine he had in a paper sack; Mrs. Jeffries and Mrs. Keebler had their ubiquitous knitting out, but their fingers were moving in slow motion as if even knitting was too much of an effort in the heat. Mr. Jamieson sat staring out the window, his expression blank as if the view outside the van was only a television screen and he was just watching the show.

The other four elderly inmates of the Sunshine Center simply sat in their seats still as statues staring straight ahead. They were probably wondering if I was ever going to get the van rolling or what was for lunch back at the center. They all looked exhausted and maybe a few were a bit tipsy from the wine they'd been sampling all morning. You had to cut them some slack, though. We'd had a busy day, we'd been waiting for Millie for almost fifteen minutes, and they wanted to go home.

I stepped up into the van. "Okay, listen up, you guys," I shouted so everyone could hear me. Old people are often hard of hearing. I discovered that fact my first day on the job at Sunshine. Eight pairs of eyes slowly fixed their attention on my face. There wasn't a spark of interest in any of them. "We're missing Millie. I can't find Millie. Any of you seen her?"

No answer.

Mr. Latrowski scratched his head. Mr. Jamieson scratched somewhere else I don't want to mention.

"Hey, I need some cooperation here. Have any of you seen Millie?"

No answer.

"Look, you guys, who was supposed to be her partner this morning? Gerald, was it you?"

Gerald Elliott, eighty-six, slowly raised his hand and grinned at me. Old people are usually very polite. I learned that my first day on the job, too. A wizened elf of a man, Gerald's hair was a wisp of white fluff on top of his head and his ears stuck out like he used them for radar. He didn't have many teeth, but what he lacked in dentures he more than made up for in fashion savvy. He wore a pink polo shirt and a pair of green plaid Bermuda shorts, knobby knees rising over white cotton knee-socks that ended in brown-tasseled loafers. His smile was endearing. He was one of my favorites.

"Okay, Gerald. When did you last see her?"

"Can't remember exactly."

"Okay, where did you last see her?"

"Beside some barrels, I think."

"That's not a lot of help, Gerald. The place is full of barrels." He put his hand down but continued to smile. He was definitely a cutie. "All right, anyone else? We can't leave until we find her and frankly, I've no clue where to start. Anyone got any ideas?"

Mrs. Grigsley, eighty-three, a little bird of a woman with a pinched face and pointy nose timidly raised her hand. "I believe

I saw her in the gift shop. But I'm not certain. I could be mistaken. I don't know. Maybe not."

Several of the others nodded in agreement. Either they'd seen Millie there, too, or they were confirming the fact that Mrs. Grigsley didn't know what the heck she was talking about.

"Well, that's something to go on," I said. "All right, listen up. Here's the deal. You guys are going to have to get out of the van and go sit on some benches in the shade. I've got to go find Millie and the van's too hot to sit in without the air conditioning running." I paused for a moment for the words to sink in. I hated to have to move them, but the thought of returning to the van to find eight cooked old people wasn't something I wanted to think about. And the alternative of leaving the van running without my supervision wasn't something I wanted to dwell on either. "Okay, let's get going."

I slid open the doors on both sides and one by one they edged out of their seats. It wasn't pretty. Several had to have their walkers brought around from the back where they'd been stowed minutes before. It was slow going, but they were troopers and kept at it. Another thing I'd learned on my first day at the center, old folks might look blank as bricks at times, but if you got their attention and got them going they could do pretty well.

Once the walker people were safely out of the way, the others, who were for the most part ambulatory, got in gear and the unloading went faster. Still it was another ten minutes before the group was finally settled on benches in the shade. Mrs. Jeffries and Mrs. Keebler got out their knitting. I gave them all one last look to make sure they were still breathing, cautioned them not to leave or speak to strangers, and went back inside in search of Millie the Missing.

Millie is my cross to bear. Close to ninety, she's still perky and she still has a lot more energy than many of the others. But sometimes her mind seems to wander. She's sweet and cooperative, but she gets lost a lot.

I searched through the gift shop in the hope that Mrs. Grigsley really did know what she was talking about, but either Millie hadn't been there or she'd already left. Next, I wandered back through the bottling areas, retracing our tour route through the building. Perhaps Millie had wandered off during the tour. I even checked in the wine tasting room to see if Millie was sampling one last Chardonnay. No luck and no Millie.

I returned to the gift shop and asked the cashiers if they'd seen a round, elderly woman wandering around by herself. I didn't want to alarm anyone because Millie usually turns up sooner or later, but I wasn't having any luck this time. They said they were sorry, but that everyone they'd seen that morning had looked round and elderly so they couldn't exactly say for sure.

Next, I checked out the little picnic area that they'd created behind the winery itself. It was an oasis of green in an otherwise tawny-brown landscape of Sierra foothill grass and oak trees. A few people were pulling out their picnic lunches and arranging them on tables, but still no Millie.

After long minutes of anxious searching I finally found Millie in the men's room calmly washing her hands at the sink. Thankfully, she wasn't washing them in the urinal.

"Hey, Millie," I said, "get a move on. We've got to leave." I tactfully tried to ignore the fact that she was the wrong sex for the facility.

She turned around and smiled at me, slowly drying her hands on a paper towel. Millie is short and round; she looks like a grandma's grandma. Her hair is tightly permed and a soft shade of aluminum gray. She goes for Koret polyester separates in shades of aqua or pink that she wears with sensible lace-up tennis shoes in coordinating colors. Today was a pink day.

"I'm sorry, dear, but I can't leave just now."

This was not the response I expected. "What do you mean you can't? The others are all outside waiting."

Millie carefully placed the paper towel in the trash bin by the sink. "I really don't think I should, dear."

"What do you mean? What's this all about?" Another thing I'd learned my first day at the Sunshine Center, seniors can get some pretty odd notions in their heads.

"Well, you see, I think there's a dead person out in the warehouse. It's a bit disconcerting. And I don't think I should just leave him there for someone else to find, do you? It wouldn't be very polite."

"A dead person? What are you talking about?"

"I saw a dead man out in the warehouse. I think maybe I should tell the police before we go."

"Wait a minute. I'm confused. Who's dead?"

"I'm afraid I don't know his name, dear."

"All right," I sighed, giving in to Millie's delusion. Discussing this was not going to get us anywhere. Better to get to the bottom of this thing so we could all go home. "Show me."

Millie took me out to the warehouse at the back of the building. It was close to where we'd begun our tour, but we hadn't gotten to look inside before. Millie opened a side door as if she knew where she was going. She led me down a long central aisle flanked on both sides by huge oak barrels some twenty feet high. And she was right. There was a dead man lying between two large vats of aging Merlot.

He lay in a pool of blood and he looked awful. He looked like he'd been pulverized. His face was a mass of dark red welts. His nose was smashed, part of his skull caved in. And it wasn't only his face. The rest of his body, what we could see of it, was covered with dark bruises about the size of a quarter.

"Yep, he definitely looks dead to me," I said, fighting the urge to be sick.

Millie flashed a smile. "See? I told you so."

We went back to the gift shop. "Excuse me, but there's a dead person in your warehouse," I said to one of the ladies. Fortunately, she turned out to be extremely concerned about having dead people lying around the winery and so was very willing to call the police.

Minutes later a squad car pulled into the parking lot with siren screaming. Millie and I retraced our steps with the police back to the warehouse and showed them the body. Then I took Millie out to sit with the other Sunshine seniors who were obviously drooping. The heat was stifling even in the shade.

I wanted to get in the van and go back to the center in the worst way, but it was a forty minute drive and I knew the police would probably want to talk to Millie, maybe me, too. The center only had the one van so the seniors and I would just have to wait where we were before we could go back. I called the center and explained the situation. Then I got water and a few snacks from the gift shop and fed the bunch on the bench. Fed and watered, they seemed able to wait a little while longer. Mrs. Jeffries and Mrs. Keebler began to knit again.

We waited over an hour while more police and the crime unit came. And despite the heat, you had to admit that it was sort of exciting. Also despite the fact that someone was dead, that is. It isn't something I'd wish on anyone, but since we couldn't go anywhere at least we had something interesting to watch and talk about. The seniors wanted to go take a look at the body, but I didn't think that was a good idea. I kept them on the bench. It wasn't easy.

Finally, a police detective in a white shirt and dark blue tie walked up. It was obvious he'd taken off his jacket because of the heat. "Are you the one who found the deceased?" he asked me.

"No, it was Millie here," I said, getting up and going over to give Millie a reassuring pat on the shoulder. "She found him while she was lost."

The others shuffled over on the bench and gave the detective room to sit down beside Millie. "You found the body?" His tone was gentle. He was a young, good-looking fellow. If he had a great grandmother, she would probably be somewhere around Millie's age.

"That's right, young man." Millie beamed at him and nodded her head.

"What time was that?"

"Well, I don't know. I forgot to wear my watch this morning, but it was quite awhile ago. It's a very nice watch, too, but I forget to wear it sometimes. It's gold-plated, I think, if that's any help."

"She had to have found him sometime between eleven and twelve," I interrupted, trying to get through the questioning before one of us fainted and fell off the bench. "We got here around eleven and we were getting ready to leave before noon." It was now past two o'clock and my little group was fading fast. They needed to eat. They needed naps. I needed a nap.

"You arrived about eleven?" the detective repeated, taking notes.

"We're on a little day trip," I explained. "An outing to a couple of wineries. We were supposed to be back to the center by twelve-thirty, but we finished our last tour and discovered Millie was lost. That's when she found the body."

"How did you find him?" the detective asked Millie.

"I just looked down and there he was."

"It appears he hasn't been dead all that long," the detective said. "Of course, until we run some tests we won't know for sure what time he died, but it's recently. Did you hear anything before you found him?"

Millie looked confused. "Why, I don't think so. My hearing isn't as good as it used to be though. They can't seem to make a hearing aid that works worth a diddly these days. I spent over four thousand dollars on the one I've got and sometimes I can't hear a thing. Have you ever heard of one that really works?"

The detective said no, he hadn't. Then he asked the others if they'd heard or seen anything suspicious. Eight heads slowly turned from side to side.

"I think I saw someone in the gift shop," Mrs. Grigsley said. "But I'm not certain. I could be mistaken. I don't know. Maybe not."

The detective stared at them for a minute or two and then smiled at me and stood up. "Well, I guess you can take them home."

The group of seniors slowly got to their feet and made their way back to the van, walkers clumping awkwardly along the sidewalk. It was slow going as usual, but I finally managed to wedge them all inside. Walkers safely stowed in the back; seatbelts securely fastened. All except Millie.

Millie was the last. As I helped her into the van I took her purse. It was heavy. "What have you got in here, Millie? Rocks?" I asked.

"Oh, no, dear," she smiled. "Only the usual things, my lipstick, my wallet, my hammer."

Borrowed Time

Dänna Suzanne Wilberg

The marquee went dark outside of the Holiday Express Hotel in El Dorado Hills. The NO VACANCY sign was turned on. It was after midnight.

Earlier that evening, Suzanne Cash had spoken of saving lives, now she was the one living on borrowed time. Her cold body struggled with consciousness. Weak snippets of memory bled through searing pain . . . the award ceremony, the applause, leaving the event on cloud nine. She was pleased with herself that the long hours of research and data gathering had paid off. But when she stopped by the pool to dig for her keys, a man had stepped out of the darkness.

"You shouldn't have meddled," he said in his thick British accent.

"I don't—" The voice was familiar, but before the threat of the situation registered, the man had spun Suzanne around and slammed her against the wrought iron fencing.

"You should've left things alone!" He seethed against her and she whimpered. Fear stole her voice; she knew he was going to kill her, but why?

The man grabbed a fist full of her hair and yanked as he pressed hard steel between her shoulder blades. A hot pain radiated through her chest just before she plunged head first to the bottom of the pool.

Familiar hands reached out from beyond the bright pool lights. Am I dead, she wondered. The hands pulled her to the water's surface and rested gently below the small of her back, but if she didn't detach herself from the pain, she would not be able to take a breath.

"Go to your happy place." Back came the advice she had given to children who were in severe pain and her mind began to search, her body relaxed. She sucked in air and let her mind float away from the flashing lights to when she was fourteen years old . . .

———

It was a grey December day. The sky was heavy with the promise of at least six more inches of snow. Suzanne's mood, bad to begin with, became worse when the school bus pulled away from the curb and splashed crud all over her suede boots. Walking home, head down, her anger mingled with depression. She hated high school. Freshman year wasn't going well and her grades were plummeting; she felt like a misfit.

By the time Suzanne looked up, it was too late. She had walked into the bumper of the car parked in front of her house. Cursing the blue Chevy for being in her way, she rubbed the goose egg forming on her kneecap and blamed God for her awful day. Just then large wet flakes fell from the sky.

"Hi," said the stranger sitting at the kitchen table. "You're all wet."

"Yep!" she said, slamming her books on the counter. Examining the tear in her tights, Suzanne's fuming resumed. "Is that your car?"

"Wow, I'd hate to see the other guy!" he laughed as he bent down to touch the throbbing bump on her knee. He was clearly vying for attention she had not intended to give, but when he touched her, he took her breath away. His touch was gentle, soothing

She figured the boy to be a senior like her oldest brother, Bill. Dressed in baggy blues, a white T-shirt and a worn quilted jacket, Suzanne had him pegged for a tough 'greaser boy'. They had a reputation for being trouble makers and weren't her type. Yet, she couldn't resist studying his face.

"Hurt much?" he asked.

Not wanting to seem obvious, she quickly diverted her eyes to the hand touching her knee. His knuckles were covered with little nicks and cuts. His unwavering stare drew her back to his handsome face. When their eyes met, she sensed kindness in his soul, generosity in his heart and a burning desire to show her who he was. Suzanne was amazed, the pain was completely gone. His eyes held her captive until her brother Bill appeared carrying a model car he had built. The boy was more interested in Suzanne.

Bill reluctantly introduced his friend as Jack, his tone of voice a signal for Suzanne to leave the kitchen and let them be. She gathered her things, about to head for her room, but Jack blocked her path. He stood in front of her with a glove dangling from his pinky finger.

"Did you drop something?" he challenged.

Suzanne took the glove, bending his finger until it hurt. His look of surprise was countered by her look of innocence as she walked past him, brushing his arm lightly. He let out a low growl at her playfulness.

––––

Pain penetrated the memory. Suzanne tried to inhale, but something was pressing on her chest. Her body rested against something hard. She stared at the stars above; the night was cold. Loud shrilly sounds whooped as she faded back into her past.

By evening, the storm had dumped three feet of snow, making it impossible to drive. The boy was stranded but didn't seem to mind. They bundled up and went outside to start shoveling.

Bill and Jack, busy piling up the last hour's accumulation on the side of the drive, didn't see Suzanne sneak around the corner and throw the first snowball. From then on, it was war. She hid behind a mound of snow closest to the back door so they couldn't get past her without getting bombarded. Before long, Jack made his way towards Suzanne, raising his arms as a shield against the onslaught of loosely packed ammunition. Laughing, he threatened to wash her face with snow once he got hold of her. She threw fluffy white stuff as fast as she could, trying to keep him at bay. When he finally reached her, he stood with his hands on his hips.

"Did you really think a little thing like you was going to stop me?" he asked. He picked up a handful of snow and made good on his promise. He moved so quickly, Suzanne was caught off guard. She had never dreamt that he would have the nerve to actually follow through with his threat. Of course, Bill was no help. After all, she had been a distraction all day.

Deciding not to resist, Suzanne let her attacker rub the ice crystals all over her face. The plan worked beautifully: as she relaxed, he did too. Once he was off balance, she pushed, sending him reeling into a deep drift of snow. He was flabbergasted! They laughed heartily as he got to his feet and surrendered for everyone to hear. He surprised her again when he grabbed her hand and pulled her through knee-deep snow to the front yard.

"Come on!" he said, like they were about to experience something fantastic. He led her to the edge of the lawn and helped her climb over the mound he and Bill had made earlier when they cleared the driveway. Turning around, they stood with their backs to the virgin snow, arms stretched out to the side.

"Ready?" he asked. It took her a moment to reply. She was caught up in the way he was looking at her. It was as if she could see her future in his eyes.

They counted to three, fell backwards and made snow angels. Looking up at the falling snow, Suzanne felt connected to God and the universe and realized that He had heard her that afternoon. She silently thanked Him for bringing this person into her life and for what she was feeling: love.

When summer came, Jack showed up for the yearly ritual of cleaning the swimming pool, earning himself an open invitation. Suzanne pretended she couldn't float on her back and needed Jack's help. He was happy to oblige. It gave them an excuse to be close. They took walks and talked about their dreams. Jack revealed his healing gift and taught Suzanne how to tap into her own healing energy. His inspiration led her to her vocation. Not only did Suzanne become an intuitive healer, she started researching the side effects of some of the drugs the children she worked with were receiving. The pharmaceutical companies didn't like her accusations, the doctors warned parents not to let her near their children, claiming she was a lunatic. Doctors feared her; she was getting results after they had given up hope—

———

Drifting in and out of consciousness, Suzanne felt like she was in a crowd of last minute shoppers on Christmas Eve, or standing in line for a rock concert. Her body was being pushed and bumped about; loud voices filled her ears. She couldn't open her eyes to see who was talking. A man named Metz-something shouted, "Did you see who shot you?"

Gasping for breath, Suzanne embraced another memory to take her away from the screaming sirens and the chaos. Her body went slack. Floating between two worlds, she remembered her first kiss—

———

She was lounging on the sofa when Jack came down the stairs. Her heart quickened. She expected to see one of her brothers follow him, but he was alone. Not wanting to seem anxious, Suzanne didn't get up. She just lay on the pillow and mumbled "hello." Instead of joining her on the couch, Jack sat on the floor, blocking her view of the TV. She tried to push him to the side so she could see, but he resisted. A tussle started and they ended up face to face. She could feel his warm breath as he looked into her eyes and whispered, "You're something else, you know that? I am always going to be here for you." He brushed the hair from her cheek. "Whenever you need me, think of this moment." He lowered his mouth to hers. The kiss was tender, their lips fit perfectly—

———

Voices, excited and hurried, pulled her from her reverie: CODE BLUE. Tears rolled down Suzanne's temples into her ears. Her body moved very quickly, causing a strobe light effect behind her fluttering lids. The voices faded as she slipped from her lucid state.

———

Bill and Jack went into the army together and served in Viet Nam. Suzanne wrote Jack letters. When the boys came home on leave, Jack asked Suzanne to marry him. Wanting to be sure of her feelings, Suzanne didn't answer right away, instead she made arrangements to meet with Jack one last time the night before he had to return to duty. When they made love that night for the first time, Suzanne prayed for time to stand still. It didn't though; time went on to become a bittersweet memory. When Jack said good-bye to Suzanne that night he promised he would come home soon. He promised he would love her until the day he died.

She never heard from him again. Until now.

———

The pain finally subsided. The voices sounded less urgent. Suzanne felt something cold running through her veins. She focused on the image behind her closed lids…

———

She was floating in a beautiful pool. There was snow on the ground, but the water was warm. She was so happy. She felt free as she looked up at the stars. The full moon shimmered in the water; she was making snow angels, her heart overflowing with love. Jack, standing nearby in his uniform, smiled. His words were very clear.

"I love you Suzanne. I'm sorry I didn't come home, but you need to listen to me. You have to be careful. They lose money when these kids get well. By proving the drugs are doing harm, you could put them out of business."

———

Suzanne slipped in and out of consciousness.

———

Suddenly she remembered Morgan. When his parents contacted Suzanne, the boy was dying. Suzanne held his hand and prayed. She told Morgan to go to a happy place, a place where pain didn't exist, a magic place where his leukemia was gone, a beautiful sanctuary where he wasn't bed-ridden.

One night Morgan's doctor came in claiming Morgan was better, his tests remarkable. The doctor talked to Suzanne extensively about her work. At first, it was hard to understand the man because of his British accent, but Suzanne expressed her concern about the medication Morgan was receiving. She related her own experience, how she herself was allergic to penicillin and that natural healing was a better alternative for her.

———

Jack spoke again, only this time he seemed so real Suzanne couldn't tell if she was dreaming.

"I'm proud of you Suzanne. You found out what the guy is up to. But be careful, you've made an enemy! Without disease, there's no need for doctors. The stuff he's putting in the water is deadly!"

———

Suzanne was confused. *What guy? What stuff? What water?*

———

"What do we have here, Dr. Wang?" A new voice with a thick British accent.

"Hi, Dr. Paulson. Caucasian female in her forties. She was found floating in the pool at the Marriot hours ago."

"Suicide?"

"No," said Wang, "gunshot wound. Barely missed the right ventricle. Laceration to the back of the head and the right temple, contusions on both wrists. Weirdest thing, her lips are blue-tinged, she's barely cyanotic, no water in the lungs, but take a look at this. Her skin is macerated; no sebum. Our girl here was in the water for quite some time, but she had to have been floating on her back."

"Strange," said Paulson. "Who found her?"

"Some guy called 911, gave her name and location. There's a Detective Metzger in the waiting room. He said they couldn't trace the call, said it was really bizarre. They could hear explosions and gunfire in the background, like the person was calling from a war zone. —Looks like she's coming to, Paulson."

"Mrs. Cash? Suzanne? Squeeze my hand if you can hear me! Mrs. Cash? Squeeze my hand! That's it. Stay with me now. Good. I'm Dr. Paulson. You're in the Mercy Folsom emergency room." Suzanne eyes flashed open. "I'll be injecting a little penicillin in your IV." He smiled. "You're going to be just fine."

About the Authors

Kathleen L. Asay, a past president of Capitol Crimes, has been reading and writing mysteries, mostly for her own enjoyment, since she discovered Nancy Drew. She has just completed her first non-mystery, a contemporary novel, *Flint House*. Kathleen has also written for regional, arts and volunteer publications. A native of Southern California, she lives in Roseville.

Patricia E. Canterbury is a native Sacramentan, an award winning poet and short story writer, novelist, philanthropist, and political scientist. She is the author of *The Secret of St. Gabriel's Tower* and *Carlotta's Secret* and is one of the founders of Capitol Crimes. Pat lives in Sacramento with her husband, Richard, the author of *Snapshots on Hell Street*. She is active with Sisters in Crime, Mystery Writers of America, Northern California Publishers and Authors, The Society of Children's Writers and Illustrators, and ZICA Creative Arts & Literary Guild. Her website: www.patmyst.com.

Juanita J. Carr, a retired registered nurse, formerly worked in the mental health field and now enjoys the extra time she has to write. Writing began for fun and pleasure at an early age when she crafted stories for grammar school classmates. Agatha Christie and Erle Stanley Gardner were her first exposure to mysteries and remain her favorite genre. She became a serious writer after joining ZICA Creative Arts & Literary Guild in 1997. A member of Capitol Crimes, she recently completed her second manuscript, a sci-fi fantasy and was a contributor to the anthology, *Life's Spices from Seasoned Sistahs.*

SM Caruthers writes in corners, on couches, waiting in cars, waiting in restaurants, on envelopes, in notebooks, in art books, on napkins, certainly on computers and long-hand, and indecipherable longhand. She writes when needing solace, company and emotional outpouring, with decision, precision and mooning about the state of things. She writes in jeans, barefoot, in e-mails and po-etry trails. Mostly, she writes. In between she reads and unpacks her hours. Suzanne is a fourth generation Cali-fornia, walker, guitar player, graduate of UC Berkeley, Resource teacher, mother of three incredible women, Hayden's grandmother and friend to an incredible musi-cian.

Gabrielle Guedet, Phd. MFT is a past president and one of the founding members of the Sacramento chapter Capitol Crimes, is an avid reader of mysteries. She is a native San Franciscan who accidentally found herself in Sac-ramento 16 years ago and has been here ever since.

Geri Spencer Hunter, a native of Iowa and a graduate of the University of Iowa's College of Nursing, won first prize for non-fiction in the Sacramento Friends of the Library writing contest in 1988 for "Coloring Book." She is also the author of *Polkadots*, a contemporary romance novel; "A Woeful Tale," a short story in *Lily Love's Café* an-thology; "Deja Vu," a short story in the anthology,

Shades of Black; and "Birth Order," a short story in the anthology *Life's Spices from Seasoned Sistahs*. She is married with children and grandchildren and lives in Sacramento, California.

R. Franklin James is a native Californian, born and raised in the San Francisco Bay Area. She is a graduate of the University of California, Berkeley in psychology. She completed the graduate program at California State University, Hayward in Public Policy. Her successful career has centered on public policy and government service including being appointed the first African-American Deputy Mayor of Los Angeles. She currently lives north of Sacramento with her husband, Leonard, Bailey, a Springer Spaniel, and Camile, the cat.

Teresa Judd, originally from Washington State and a graduate of the University of Washington in Far Eastern studies, now lives in the Sacramento area and is employed as a manufacturer's representative in the gift industry. Previous employment has taken her through a government position in Washington D. C., public relations and advertising positions in the Philadelphia-South Jersey area and book sales in northern California. She is also a member of Romance Writers of America and hopes to put her experiences to good use in the newly begun writing career.

Norma Lehr is a multi-genre author of short stories and mid-grade ghost stories. She is a former nurse and health food store owner from the Bay Area. Norma now lives in Auburn, California in the beautiful Sierra foothills and is currently working on an adult traditional mystery series. Her dark fantasy suspense novel, *Dark Maiden*, was published by Juno Books, an imprint of Wildside Press, in 2007. Her website is www.normalehr.com.

Nan Mahon is a freelance writer, author and award-winning journalist. Her articles appear regularly in the *Sacramento Bee* and *Senior Magazine*. Because of her active role in the Sacramento area writers and arts community, Senior Magazine named her a Woman of Influence in March 2007. She lives in Elk Grove, California and was the Lifestyle editor of the Elk Grove Citizen for ten years. Her books include, *Junkyard Blues*, *Pink Pears and Irish Whiskey*, and *Hard Times and Honeysuckle*.

Joyce Mason started writing and publishing poetry in the '70s. Later, moonlighting as an astrologer from her government day job, she switched to prose and sky hints with articles in *The Mountain Astrologer* and similar publications. Still, she wrote plenty working for the State for 31 years. Mystery was an accidental discovery, while conjuring up a book under pressure of a contest deadline. Thanks to Janet Evanovich, Joyce realized a romantic whodunit could be molded into a cozy mystery, her back burner project while she wraps up her first memoir, *Hot Flashbacks, Cool Insights*. Her website: www.joycemason.com and her blog is http://hotflashbackscoolinsights.blogspot.com/.

Maggie McMillen is the pen name of a Capitol Crime member who retired and relocated to Arnold, California from the Bay Area in June 1994 after working as a publicist and advertising account executive for twenty years. Born in Portland and educated at Oregon State University, she had developed client press releases that appeared in major print media in the U. S. and Great Britain. Her client list included businesses, hotels, restaurants, and authors. She booked clients on television and radio and accompanied some on book tours. She published poetry in anthologies in 1998-1999. She's a member of Blue Coyote Writers of Calaveras as well as Sisters in Crime.

Cindy Sample received her first writing award at the impressionable age of eight. She astutely determined, however, that she should focus on a job with a weekly paycheck and began a 28 year career in the mortgage industry, rising from receptionist to President/CEO of a national mortgage banking company. She was awarded Boss of the Year by the Sacramento Chapter of the Association of Professional Women in 2000. In 2001, Cindy decided she wanted to focus on murder, not mortgage. As a single mother/CEO, she had enough material for a series of novels. She is currently seeking a publisher for *Dying for a Date*.

Linda Joy Singleton reads, writes and collects juvenile series books from a first edition Nancy Drew to the latest YA series. She's the author of several YA series: The Seer series featuring a psychic teen, Regeneration dealing with cloned teens, and the Dead Girl series launching in 2008. She has advice for writers on her website www.LindaJoySingleton.com. Linda Joy grew up in

Sacramento County and now lives in the foothills with her husband and a menagerie of pets.

Nancy Streukens was an unpublished writer prior to this anthology, with a career in banking and technical writing. She's written two novels, a Regency romance several years ago and more recently a cozy murder mystery set in rural Iowa farm country. Nancy is currently working on her second mystery, a sequel to the first. She's been in love with all things English and mysteries ever since she discovered Georgette Heyer's novels in her twenties.

Dänna Suzanne Wilberg, a stay-at-home mom, viewed every day as a mystery: "The Missing Sock," "The Hairless Doll," "The Writing on the Wall." Her creative juices flow profusely at three a.m. While other moms sent around starter loaves of sourdough bread, Danna wrote mystery stories on her computer to send to other insomniacs, the story added to as it was sent back and forth. Her children now grown, Danna joined a writers' group, became serious about writing and turned one of her short stories into a full length novel, *The Red Chair*.